THE RUNAWAY SKYSCRAPER

AND OTHER TALES FROM THE PULPS

MORE WILDSIDE CLASSICS

THE RUNAWAY SKYSCRAPER

SKYSCRAPER

AND OTHER TALES FROM THE PULPS

MURRAY LEINSTER

WILDSIDE PRESS

THE RUNAWAY SKYSCRAPER
AND OTHER TALES FROM THE PULPS

"The Runaway Skyscraper" originally appeared in the February 22, 1919 issue of *Argosy* magazine. "The Gallery Gods" originally appeared in *Argosy All-Weekly*, August 21, 1920. "The Street of Magnificent Dreams" originally appeared in *Argosy All-Story Weekly*, August 5, 1922. "Nerve" originally appeared in *Argosy All-Story Weekly*, June 4, 1921. "Morale" originally appeared in *Astounding Stories*, December 1931. "Grooves" originally appeared in *All-Story Magazine*. "Footprints in the Snow" originally appeared in *All-Story Magazine*. June 7, 1919.

CONTENTS

THE RUNAWAY SKYSCRAPER

I.

The whole thing started when the clock on the Metropolitan Tower began to run backward. It was not a graceful proceeding. The hands had been moving onward in their customary deliberate fashion, slowly and thoughtfully, but suddenly the people in the offices near the clock's face heard an ominous creaking and groaning. There was a slight, hardly discernible shiver through the tower, and then something gave with a crash. The big hands on the clock began to move backward.

Immediately after the crash all the creaking and groaning ceased, and instead, the usual quiet again hung over everything. One or two of the occupants of the upper offices put their heads out into the halls, but the elevators were running as usual, the lights were burning, and all seemed calm and peaceful. The clerks and stenographers went back to their ledgers and typewriters, the business callers returned to the discussion of their errands, and the ordinary course of business was resumed.

Arthur Chamberlain was dictating a letter to Estelle Woodward, his sole stenographer. When the crash came he paused, listened, and then resumed his task.

It was not a difficult one. Talking to Estelle Woodward was at no time an onerous duty, but it must be admitted that Arthur Chamberlain found it difficult to keep his conversation strictly upon his business.

He was at this time engaged in dictating a letter to his principal creditors, the Gary & Milton Company, explaining that their demand for the immediate payment of the installment then due upon his office furniture was untimely and unjust. A young and budding engineer in New York never has too much money, and when he is young as Arthur Chamberlain was, and as fond of pleasant company, and not too fond of economizing, he is liable to find all demands for payment untimely and he usually considers them unjust as well. Arthur finished dictating the letter and sighed.

"Miss Woodward," he said regretfully, "I am afraid I shall never make a successful man."

Miss Woodward shook her head vaguely. She did not seem to take his remark very seriously, but then, she had learned never to take any of his remarks seriously. She had been puzzled at first by his manner of treating everything with a half joking pessimism, but now ignored it.

She was interested in her own problems. She had suddenly decided that she was going to be an old maid, and it bothered her. She had discovered that she did not like any one well enough to marry, and she was in her twenty-second year.

She was not a native of New York, and the few young men she had met there she did not care for. She had regretfully decided she was too finicky, too fastidious, but could not seem to help herself. She could not understand their absorption in boxing and baseball and she did not like the way they danced.

She had considered the matter and decided that she would have to reconsider her former opinion of women who did not marry. Heretofore she had thought there must be something the matter with them. Now she believed that she would come to their own estate, and probably for the same reason. She could not fall in love and she wanted to.

She read all the popular novels and thrilled at the love scenes contained in them, but when any of the young men she knew became in the slightest degree sentimental she found herself bored, and disgusted with herself for being bored. Still, she could not help it, and was struggling to reconcile herself to a life without romance.

She was far too pretty for that, of course, and Arthur Chamberlain often longed to tell her how pretty she really was, but her abstracted air held him at arms' length.

He lay back at ease in his swivel chair and considered, looking at her with unfeigned pleasure. She did not notice it, for she was so much absorbed in her own thoughts that she rarely noticed anything he said or did when they were not in the line of her duties.

"Miss Woodward," he repeated, "I said I think I'll never make a successful man. Do you know what that means?"

She looked at him mutely, polite inquiry in her eyes.

"It means," he said gravely, "that I'm going broke. Unless something turns up in the next three weeks, or a month at the latest, I'll have to get a job."

"And that means —" she asked.

"All this will go to pot," he explained with a sweeping gesture. "I thought I'd better tell you as much in advance as I could."

"You mean you're going to give up your office — and me?" she asked, a little alarmed.

"Giving up you will be the harder of the two," he said with a smile, "but that's what it means. You'll have no difficulty finding a new place, with three weeks in which to look for one, but I'm sorry."

"I'm sorry, too, Mr. Chamberlain," she said, her brow puckered.

She was not really frightened, because she knew she could get another position, but she became aware of rather more regret than she had expected.

There was silence for a moment.

"Jove!" said Arthur, suddenly. "It's getting dark, isn't it?"

It was. It was growing dark with unusual rapidity. Arthur went to his window, and looked out.

"Funny," he remarked in a moment or two. "Things don't look just right, down there, somehow. There are very few people about."

He watched in growing amazement. Lights came on in the streets below, but none of the buildings lighted up. It grew darker and darker.

"It shouldn't be dark at this hour!" Arthur exclaimed.

Estelle went to the window by his side.

"It looks awfully queer," she agreed. "It must be an eclipse or something."

They heard doors open in the hall outside, and Arthur ran out. The halls were beginning to fill with excited people.

"What on earth's the matter?" asked a worried stenographer.

"Probably an eclipse," replied Arthur. "Only it's odd we didn't read about it in the papers."

He glanced along the corridor. No one else seemed better informed than he, and he went back into his office.

Estelle turned from the window as he appeared.

"The streets are deserted," she said in a puzzled tone. "What's the matter? Did you hear?"

Arthur shook his head and reached for the telephone.

"I'll call up and find out," he said confidently. He held the receiver to his ear. "What the —" he exclaimed. "Listen to this!"

A small-sized roar was coming from the receiver. Arthur hung up and turned a blank face upon Estelle.

"Look!" she said suddenly, and pointed out of the window.

All the city was now lighted up, and such of the signs as they could see were brilliantly illumined. They watched in silence. The streets once more seemed filled with vehicles. They darted along, their headlamps lighting up the roadway brilliantly. There was, however, something strange even about their motion. Arthur and Estelle watched in growing amazement and perplexity.

"Are — are you seeing what I am seeing?" asked Estelle breathlessly. "*I see them going backward!*"

Arthur watched, and collapsed into a chair.

"For the love of Mike!" he exclaimed softly.

II.

He was roused by another exclamation from Estelle.

"It's getting light again," she said.

Arthur rose and went eagerly to the window. The darkness was becoming less intense, but in a way Arthur could hardly credit.

Far to the west, over beyond the Jersey hills — easily visible from the height at which Arthur's office was located — a faint light appeared in the sky, grew stronger and then took on a reddish tint. That, in turn, grew deeper, and at last the sun appeared, rising unconcernedly *in the west.*

Arthur gasped. The streets below continued to be thronged with people and motorcars. The sun was traveling with extraordinary rapidity. It rose overhead, and as if by magic the streets were thronged with people. Every one seemed to be running at top speed. The few teams they saw moved at a breakneck pace — backward! In spite of the suddenly topsyturvy state of affairs there seemed to be no accidents.

Arthur put his hands to his head.

"Miss Woodward," he said pathetically, "I'm afraid I've gone crazy. Do you see the same things I do?"

Estelle nodded. Her eyes wide open.

"What *is* the matter?" she asked helplessly.

She turned again to the window. The square was almost empty once more. The motorcars still traveling about the streets were going so swiftly they were hardly visible. Their speed seemed to increase steadily. Soon it was almost impossible to distinguish them, and only a grayish blur marked their paths along Fifth Avenue and Twenty-Third Street.

It grew dusk, and then rapidly dark. As their office was on the western side of the building they could not see that the sun had sunk in the east, but subconsciously they realized that this must be the case.

In silence they watched the panorama grow black except for the streetlamps, remain thus for a time, and then suddenly spring into brilliantly illuminated activity.

Again this lasted for a little while, and the west once more began to glow. The sun rose somewhat more hastily from the Jersey hills and began to soar overhead, but very soon darkness fell again. With hardly an interval the city became illuminated, and then the west grew red once more.

"Apparently," said Arthur, steadying his voice with a conscious effort, "there's been a cataclysm somewhere, the direction of the earth's rotation has been reversed, and its speed immensely increased. It seems to take only about five minutes for a rotation now."

As he spoke darkness fell for the third time. Estelle turned from the window with a white face.

"What's going to happen?" she cried.

"I don't know," answered Arthur. "The scientist fellows tell us if the earth were to spin fast enough the centrifugal force would throw us all off into space. Perhaps that's what's going to happen."

Estelle sank into a chair and stared at him, appalled. There was a sudden explosion behind them. With a start, Estelle jumped to her feet and turned. A little gilt clock over her typewriter-desk lay in fragments. Arthur hastily glanced at his own watch.

"Great bombs and little cannonballs!" he shouted. "Look at this!"

His watch trembled and quivered in his hand. The hands were going around so swiftly it was impossible to watch the minute hand, and the hour hand traveled like the wind.

While they looked, it made two complete revolutions. In one of them the glory of daylight had waxed, waned, and vanished. In the other, darkness reigned except for the glow from the electric light overhead.

There was a sudden tension and catch in the watch. Arthur dropped it instantly. It flew to pieces before it reached the floor.

"If you've got a watch," Arthur ordered swiftly, "stop it this instant!"

Estelle fumbled at her wrist. Arthur tore the watch from her hand and threw open the case. The machinery inside was going so swiftly it was hardly visible; Relentlessly, Arthur jabbed a penholder in the works. There was a sharp click, and the watch was still.

Arthur ran to the window. As he reached it the sun rushed up, day lasted a moment, there was darkness, and then the sun appeared again.

"Miss Woodward!" Arthur ordered suddenly, "look at the ground!"

Estelle glanced down. The next time the sun flashed into view she gasped.

The ground was white with snow!

"What *has* happened?" she demanded, terrified. "Oh, what *has* happened?"

Arthur fumbled at his chin awkwardly, watching the astonishing panorama outside. There was hardly any distinguishing between the times the sun was up and the times it was below now, as the darkness and light followed each other so swiftly the effect was the same as one of the old flickering motion pictures.

As Arthur watched, this effect became more pronounced. The tall Fifth Avenue Building across the way began to disintegrate. In a moment, it seemed, there was only a skeleton there. Then that vanished, story by story. A great cavity in the earth appeared, and then another building became visible, a smaller, brownstone, unimpressive structure.

With bulging eyes Arthur stared across the city. Except for the flickering, he could see almost clearly now.

He no longer saw the sun rise and set. There was merely a streak of unpleasantly brilliant light across the sky. Bit by bit, building by building, the city began to disintegrate and become replaced by smaller, dingier buildings. In a little while those began to disappear and leave gaps where they vanished.

Arthur strained his eyes and looked far downtown. He saw a forest of masts and spars along the waterfront for a moment and when he turned his eyes again to the scenery near him it was almost barren of houses, and what few showed were mean, small residences, apparently set in the midst of farms and plantations.

Estelle was sobbing.

"Oh, Mr. Chamberlain," she cried. "What is the matter? What has happened?"

Arthur had lost his fear of what their fate would be in his absorbing interest in what he saw. He was staring out of the window, wide eyed, lost in the sight before him. At Estelle's cry, however, he reluctantly left the window and patted her shoulder awkwardly.

"I don't know how to explain it," he said uncomfortably, "but it's obvious that my first surmise was all wrong. The speed of the earth's rotation can't have been increased, because if it had to the extent we see, we'd have been thrown off into space long ago. But — have you read anything about the Fourth Dimension?"

Estelle shook her head hopelessly.

"Well, then, have you ever read anything by Wells? The 'Time Machine,' for instance?"

Again she shook her head.

"I don't know how I'm going to say it so you'll understand, but time is just as much a dimension as length and breadth. From what I can judge, I'd say there has been an earthquake, and the ground has settled a little with our building on it, only instead of settling down toward the center of the earth, or sidewise, it's settled in this fourth dimension."

"But what does that mean?" asked Estelle uncomprehendingly.

"If the earth had settled down, we'd have been lower. If it had settled to one side, we'd have been moved one way or another, but as it's settled back in the Fourth Dimension, we're going back in time."

"Then —"

"We're in a runaway skyscraper, bound for some time back before the discovery of America!"

III.

It was very still in the office. Except for the flickering outside everything seemed very much as usual. The electric light burned steadily, but Estelle was sobbing with fright and Arthur was trying vainly to console her.

"Have I gone crazy?" she demanded between her sobs.

"Not unless I've gone mad, too," said Arthur soothingly. The excitement had quite a soothing effect upon him. He had ceased to feel afraid, but was simply waiting to see what had happened. "We're way back before the founding of New York now, and still going strong."

"Are you sure that's what has happened?"

"If you'll look outside," he suggested, "you'll see the seasons following each other in reverse order. One moment the snow covers all the ground, then you catch a glimpse of autumn foliage, then summer follows, and next spring."

Estelle glanced out of the window and covered her eyes.

"Not a house," she said despairingly. "Not a building. Nothing, nothing, nothing!"

Arthur slipped his arm about her and patted hers comfortingly.

"It's all right," he reassured her. "We'll bring up presently, and there we'll be. There's nothing to be afraid of."

She rested her head on his shoulder and sobbed hopelessly for a little while longer, but presently quieted. Then, suddenly, realizing that Arthur's arm was about her and that she was crying on his shoulder, she sprang away, blushing crimson.

Arthur walked to the window.

"Look there!" he exclaimed, but it was too late. "I'll swear to it I saw the Half Moon, Hudson's ship," he declared excitedly. "We're way back now, and don't seem to be slacking up, either."

Estelle came to the window by his side. The rapidly changing scene before her made her gasp. It was no longer possible to distinguish night from day.

A wavering streak, moving first to the right and then to the left, showed where the sun flashed across the sky.

"What makes the sun wabble so?" she asked.

"Moving north and south of the equator," Arthur explained casually. "When it's farthest south — to the left — there's always snow on the ground. When it's farthest right it's summer. See how green it is?"

A few moments' observation corroborated his statement.

"I'd say," Arthur remarked reflectively, "that it takes about fifteen seconds for the sun to make the round trip from farthest north to farthest south." He felt his pulse. "Do you know the normal rate of the heartbeat? We can judge time that way. A clock will go all to pieces, of course."

"Why did your watch explode — and the clock?"

"Running forward in time unwinds a clock, doesn't it?" asked Arthur. "It follows, of course, that when you move it backward in time it winds up. When you move it too far back, you wind it so tightly that the spring just breaks to pieces."

He paused a moment, his fingers on his pulse.

"Yes, it takes about fifteen seconds for all the four seasons to pass. That means we're going backward in time about four years a minute. If we go on at this rate another hour we'll be back in the time of the Northmen, and will be able to tell if they did discover America, after all."

"Funny we don't hear any noises," Estelle observed. She had caught some of Arthur's calmness.

"It passes so quickly that though our ears hear it, we don't separate the sounds. If you'll notice, you do hear a sort of humming. It's very high pitched, though."

Estelle listened, but could hear nothing.

"No matter," said Arthur. "It's probably a little higher than your ears will catch. Lots of people can't hear a bat squeak."

"I never could," said Estelle. "Out in the country, where I come from, other people could hear them, but I couldn't."

They stood a while in silence, watching.

"When are we going to stop?" asked Estelle uneasily. "It seems as if we're going to keep on indefinitely."

"I guess we'll stop all right," Arthur reassured her. "It's obvious that whatever it was, only affected our own building, or we'd see some other one with us. It looks like a fault or a flaw in the rock the building rests on. And that can only give so far."

Estelle was silent for a moment.

"Oh, I can't be sane!" she burst out semihysterically. "This can't be happening!"

"You aren't crazy," said Arthur sharply. "You're sane as I am. Just something queer is happening. Buck up. Say your multiplication tables. Say anything you know. Say something sensible and you'll know you're all right. But don't get frightened now. There'll be plenty to get frightened about later."

The grimness in his tone alarmed Estelle.

"What are you afraid of?" she asked quickly.

"Time enough to worry when it happens," Arthur retorted briefly.

"You — you aren't afraid we'll go back before the beginning of the world, are you?" asked Estelle in sudden access of fright.

Arthur shook his head.

"Tell me," said Estelle more quietly, getting a grip on herself. "I won't mind. But please tell me."

Arthur glanced at her. Her face was pale, but there was more resolution in it than he had expected to find.

"I'll tell you, then," he said reluctantly. "We're going back a little faster than we were, and the flaw seems to be a deeper one than I thought. At the roughest kind of an estimate, we're all of a thousand years before the discovery of America now, and I think nearer three or four. And we're gaining speed all the time. So, though I am as sure as I can be sure of anything that we'll stop this cave-in eventually, I don't know where. It's like a crevasse in the earth opened by an earthquake which may be only a few feet deep, or it may be hundreds of yards, or even a mile or two. We started off smoothly. We're going at a terrific rate. *What will happen when we stop?*"

Estelle caught her breath.

"What?" she asked quietly.

"I don't know," said Arthur in an irritated tone, to cover his apprehension. "How could I know?"

Estelle turned from him to the window again.

"Look!" she said, pointing.

The flickering had begun again. While they stared, hope springing up once more in their hearts, it became more pronounced. Soon they could distinctly see the difference between day and night.

They were slowing up! The white snow on the ground remained there for an appreciable time, autumn lasted quite a while. They could catch the flashes of the sun as it made its revolutions now, instead of its seeming like a ribbon of fire. At last day lasted all of fifteen or twenty minutes.

It grew longer and longer. Then half an hour, then an hour. The sun wavered in midheaven and was still.

Far below them, the watchers in the tower of the skyscraper saw trees swaying and bending in the wind. Though there was not a house or a habitation to be seen and a dense forest covered all of Manhattan Island, such of the world as they could see looked normal. Wherever or rather in whatever epoch of time they were, they had arrived.

IV.

Arthur caught at Estelle's arm and the two made a dash for the elevators. Fortunately one was standing still, the door open, on their floor. The elevator-boy had deserted his post and was looking with all the rest of the occupants of the building at the strange landscape that surrounded them.

No sooner had the pair reached the car, however, than the boy came hurrying along the corridor, three or four other people following him also at a run. Without a word the boy rushed inside, the others crowded after him, and the car shot downward, all of the newcomers panting from their sprint.

Theirs was the first car to reach the bottom. They rushed out and to the western door.

Here, where they had been accustomed to see Madison Square spread out before them, a clearing of perhaps half an acre in extent showed itself. Where their eyes instinctively looked for the dark bronze fountain, near which soapbox orators aforetime held sway, they saw a tent, a wigwam of hides and bark gaily painted. And before the wigwam were two or three brown-skinned Indians, utterly petrified with astonishment.

Behind the first wigwam were others, painted like the first with daubs of brightly colored clay. From them, too, Indians issued, and stared in incredulous amazement, their eyes growing wider and wider. When the group of white people confronted the Indians there was a moment's deathlike silence. Then, with a wild yell, the redskins broke and ran, not stopping to gather together their belongings, nor pausing for even a second glance at the weird strangers who invaded their domain.

Arthur took two or three deep breaths of the fresh air and found himself even then comparing its quality with that of the city. Estelle stared about her with unbelieving eyes. She turned and saw the great bulk of the office building behind her, then faced this small clearing with a virgin forest on its farther side.

She found herself trembling from some undefined cause. Arthur glanced at her. He saw the trembling and knew she would have a fit of nerves in a moment if something did not come up demanding instant attention.

"We'd better take a look at this village," he said in an offhand voice. "We can probably find out how long ago it is from the weapons and so on."

He grasped her arm firmly and led her in the direction of the tents. The other people, left behind, displayed their emotions in different ways. Two or three of them — women — sat frankly down on the steps and indulged in tears of bewilderment, fright and relief in a peculiar combination defying analysis. Two or three of the men swore, in shaken voices.

Meantime, the elevators inside the building were rushing and clanging, and the hall filled with a white-faced mob, desperately anxious to find out what had happened and why. The people poured out of the door and stared about blankly. There was a peculiar expression of doubt on every one of their faces. Each one was asking himself if he were awake, and having proved that by pinches, openly administered, the next query was whether they had gone mad.

Arthur led Estelle cautiously among the tents.

The village contained about a dozen wigwams. Most of them were made of strips of birch bark, cleverly overlapping each other, the seams cemented with gum. All had hide flaps for doors, and one or two were built almost entirely of hides, sewed together with strips of sinew.

Arthur made only a cursory examination of the village. His principal motive in taking Estelle there was to give her some mental occupation to ward off the reaction from the excitement of the cataclysm.

He looked into one or two of the tents and found merely couches of hides, with minor domestic utensils scattered about. He brought from one tent a bow and quiver of arrows. The workmanship was good, but very evidently the maker had no knowledge of metal tools.

Arthur's acquaintance with archeological subjects was very slight, but he observed that the arrowheads were chipped, and not rubbed smooth. They were attached to the shafts with strips of gut or tendon.

Arthur was still pursuing his investigation when a sob from Estelle made him stop and look at her.

"Oh, what are we going to do?" she asked tearfully. "What *are* we going to do? Where are we?"

"You mean, *when* are we," Arthur corrected with a grim smile. "I don't know. Way back before the discovery of America, though. You can see in everything in the village that there isn't a trace of European civilization. I suspect that we are several thousand years back. I can't tell, of course, but this pottery makes me think so. See this bowl?"

He pointed to a bowl of red clay lying on the ground before one of the wigwams.

"If you'll look, you'll see that it isn't really pottery at all. It's a basket that was woven of reeds and then smeared with clay to make it fire-resisting. The people who made that didn't know about baking clay to make it stay put. When America was discovered nearly all the tribes knew something about pottery."

"But what are we going to do?" Estelle tearfully insisted.

"We're going to muddle along as well as we can," answered Arthur cheerfully, "until we can get back to where we started from. Maybe the people back in the twentieth century can send a relief party after us. When the skyscraper vanished it must have left a hole of some sort, and it may be possible for them to follow us down."

"If that's so," said Estelle quickly, "why can't we climb up it without waiting for them to come after us?"

Arthur scratched his head. He looked across the clearing at the skyscraper. It seemed to rest very solidly on the ground. He looked up. The sky seemed normal.

"To tell the truth," he admitted, "there doesn't seem to be any hole. I said that more to cheer you up than anything else."

Estelle clenched her hands tightly and took a grip on herself.

"Just tell me the truth," she said quietly. "I was rather foolish, but tell me what you honestly think."

Arthur eyed her keenly.

"In that case," he said reluctantly, "I'll admit we're in a pretty bad fix. I don't know what has happened, how it happened, or anything about it. I'm just going to keep on going until I see a way clear to get out of this mess. There are two thousand of us people, more or less, and among all of us we must be able to find a way out."

Estelle had turned very pale.

"We're in no great danger from Indians," went on Arthur thoughtfully, "or from anything else that I know of — except one thing."

"What is that?" asked Estelle quickly.

Arthur shook his head and led her back toward the sky-scraper, which was now thronged with the people from all the floors who had come down to the ground and were standing excitedly about the concourse asking each other what had happened.

Arthur led Estelle to one of the corners.

"Wait for me here," he ordered. "I'm going to talk to this crowd."

He pushed his way through until he could reach the confectionery and news-stand in the main hallway. Here he climbed up on the counter and shouted:

"People, listen to me! I'm going to tell you what's happened!"

In an instant there was dead silence. He found himself the center of a sea of white faces, every one contorted with fear and anxiety.

"To begin with," he said confidently, "there's nothing to be afraid of. We're going to get back to where we started from! I don't know how, yet, but we'll do it. Don't get frightened. Now I'll tell you what's happened."

He rapidly sketched out for them, in words as simple as he could make them, his theory that a flaw in the rock on which the foundations rested had developed and let the skyscraper sink, not downward, but into the Fourth Dimension.

"I'm an engineer," he finished. "What nature can do, we can imitate. Nature let us into this hole. We'll climb out. In the mean time, matters are serious. We needn't be afraid of not getting back. We'll do that. What we've got to fight is — starvation!"

* * *

V.

"We've got to fight starvation, and we've got to beat it," Arthur continued doggedly. "I'm telling you this right at the outset, because I want you to begin right at the beginning and pitch in to help. We have very little food and a lot of us to eat it. First, I want some volunteers to help with rationing. Next, I want every ounce of food in this place put under guard where it can be served to those who need it most. Who will help out with this?"

The swift succession of shocks had paralyzed the faculties of most of the people there, but half a dozen moved forward. Among them was a single gray-haired man with an air of accustomed authority. Arthur recognized him as the president of the bank on the ground floor.

"I don't know who you are or if you're right in saying what has happened," said the gray-haired man. "But I see something's got to be done, and — well, for the time being I'll take your word for what that is. Later on we'll thrash this matter out."

Arthur nodded. He bent over and spoke in a low voice to the gray-haired man, who moved away.

"Grayson, Walters, Terhune, Simpson, and Forsythe, come here," the gray-haired man called at a doorway.

A number of men began to press dazedly toward him. Arthur resumed his harangue.

"You people — those of you who aren't too dazed to think — are remembering there's a restaurant in the building and no need to starve. You're wrong. There are nearly two thousand of us here. That means six thousand meals a day. We've got to have nearly ten tons of food a day, and we've got to have it at once."

"Hunt?" some one suggested.

"I saw Indians," some one else shouted. "Can we trade with them?"

"We can hunt and we can trade with the Indians," Arthur admitted, "but we need food by the ton — by the ton, people! The Indians don't store up supplies, and, besides, they're much too scattered to have a surplus for us. But we've got to have food. Now, how many of you know anything about hunting, fishing, trapping, or any possible way of getting food?"

There were a few hands raised — pitifully few. Arthur saw Estelle's hand up.

"Very well," he said. "Those of you who raised your hands then come with me up on the second floor and we'll talk it over.

The rest of you try to conquer your fright, and don't go outside for a while. We've got some things to attend to before it will be quite safe for you to venture out. And keep away from the restaurant. There are armed guards over that food. Before we pass it out indiscriminately, we'll see to it there's more for tomorrow and the next day."

He stepped down from the counter and moved toward the stairway. It was not worth while to use the elevator for the ride of only one floor. Estelle managed to join him, and they mounted the steps together.

"Do you think we'll pull through all right?" she asked quietly.

"We've got to!" Arthur told her, setting his chin firmly. "We've simply got to."

The gray-haired president of the bank was waiting for them at the top of the stairs.

"My name is Van Deventer," he said, shaking hands with Arthur, who gave his own name.

"Where shall our emergency council sit?" he asked.

"The bank has a board room right over the safety vault. I dare say we can accommodate everybody there — everybody in the council, anyway."

Arthur followed into the board-room, and the others trooped in after him.

"I'm just assuming temporary leadership," Arthur explained, "because it's imperative some things be done at once. Later on we can talk about electing officials to direct our activities. Right now we need food. How many of you can shoot?"

About a quarter of the hands were raised. Estelle's was among the number.

"And how many are fishermen?"

A few more went up.

"What do the rest of you do?"

There was a chorus of "gardener," "I have a garden in my yard," "I grow peaches in New Jersey," and three men confessed that they raised chickens as a hobby.

"We'll want you gardeners in a little while. Don't go yet. But the most important are huntsmen and fishermen. Have any of you weapons in your offices?"

A number had revolvers, but only one man had a shotgun and shells. "I was going on my vacation this afternoon straight from the office," he explained, "and have all my vacation tackle."

"Good man!" Arthur exclaimed. "You'll go after the heavy game."

"With a shotgun?" the sportsman asked, aghast.

"If you get close to them a shotgun will do as well as anything, and we can't waste a shell on every bird or rabbit. Those shells of yours are precious. You other fellows will have to turn fishermen for a while. Your pistols are no good for hunting."

"The watchmen at the bank have riot guns," said Van Deventer, "and there are one or two repeating-rifles there. I don't know about ammunition."

"Good! I don't mean about the ammunition, but about the guns. We'll hope for the ammunition. You fishermen get to work to improvise tackle out of anything you can get hold of. Will you do that?"

A series of nods answered his question.

"Now for the gardeners. You people will have to roam through the woods in company with the hunters and locate anything in the way of edibles that grows. Do all of you know what wild plants look like? I mean wild fruits and vegetables that are good to eat."

A few of them nodded, but the majority looked dubious. The consensus of opinion seemed to be that they would try. Arthur seemed a little discouraged.

"I guess you're the man to tell about the restaurant," Van Deventer said quietly. "And as this is the food commission, or something of that sort, everybody here will be better for hearing it. Anyway, everybody will have to know it before night. I took over the restaurant as you suggested, and posted some of the men from the bank that I knew I could trust about the doors. But there was hardly any use in doing it."

"The restaurant stocks up in the afternoon, as most of its business is in the morning and at noon. It only carries a day's stock of foodstuffs, and the — the cataclysm, or whatever it was, came at three o'clock. There is practically nothing in the place. We couldn't make sandwiches for half the women that are caught with us, let alone the men. Everybody will go hungry tonight. There will be no breakfast tomorrow, nor anything to eat until we either make arrangements with the Indians for some supplies or else get food for ourselves."

Arthur leaned his jaw on his hand and considered. A slow flush crept over his cheek. He was getting his fighting blood up.

At school, when he began to flush slowly his schoolmates had known the symptom and avoided his wrath. Now he was growing angry with mere circumstances, but it would be none the less unfortunate for those circumstances.

"Well," he said at last deliberately, "we've got to — What's that?"

There was a great creaking and groaning. Suddenly a sort of vibration was felt under foot. The floor began to take on a slight slant.

"Great Heaven!" some one cried. "The building's turning over and we'll be buried in the ruins!"

The tilt of the floor became more pronounced. An empty chair slid to one end of the room. There was a crash.

VI.

Arthur woke to find some one tugging at his shoulders, trying to drag him from beneath the heavy table, which had wedged itself across his feet and pinned him fast, while a flying chair had struck him on the head and knocked him unconscious.

"Oh, come and help," Estelle's voice was calling deliberately. "Somebody come and help! He's caught in here!"

She was sobbing in a combination of panic and some unknown emotion.

"Help me, please!" she gasped, then her voice broke despondently, but she never ceased to tug ineffectually at Chamberlain, trying to drag him out of the mass of wreckage.

Arthur moved a little, dazedly.

"Are you alive?" she called anxiously. "Are you alive? Hurry, oh, hurry and wriggle out. The building's falling to pieces!"

"I'm all right," Arthur said weakly. "You get out before it all comes down."

"I won't leave you," she declared "Where are you caught? Are you badly hurt? Hurry, please hurry!"

Arthur stirred, but could not loosen his feet. He half rolled over, and the table moved as if it had been precariously balanced, and slid heavily to one side. With Estelle still tugging at him, he managed to get to his feet on the slanting floor and stared about him.

Arthur continued to stare about.

"No danger," he said weakly. "Just the floor of the one room gave way. The aftermath of the rock-flaw."

He made his way across the splintered flooring and piled-up chairs.

"We're on top of the safe-deposit vault," he said. "That's why we didn't fall all the way to the floor below. I wonder how we're going to get down?"

Estelle followed him, still frightened for fear of the building falling upon them. Some of the long floorboards stretched over the edge of the vault and rested on a tall, bronze grating that protected the approach to the massive strongbox. Arthur tested them with his foot.

"They seem to be pretty solid," he said tentatively.

His strength was coming back to him every moment. He had been no more than stunned. He walked out on the planking to the bronze grating and turned.

"If you don't get dizzy, you might come on," he said. "We can swing down the grille here to the floor."

Estelle followed gingerly and in a moment they were safely below. The corridor was quite empty.

"When the crash came," Estelle explained, her voice shaking with the reaction from her fear of a moment ago, "every one thought the building was coming to pieces, and ran out. I'm afraid they've all run away."

"They'll be back in a little while," Arthur said quietly.

They went along the big marble corridor to the same western door, out of which they had first gone to see the Indian village. As they emerged into the sunlight they met a few of the people who had already recovered from their panic and were returning.

A crowd of respectable size gathered in a few moments, all still pale and shaken, but coming back to the building which was their refuge. Arthur leaned wearily against the cold stone. It seemed to vibrate under his touch. He turned quickly to Estelle.

"Feel this," he exclaimed.

She did so.

"I've been wondering what that rumble was," she said. "I've been hearing it ever since we landed here, but didn't understand where it came from."

"You hear a rumble?" Arthur asked, puzzled. "I can't hear anything."

"It isn't as loud as it was, but I hear it," Estelle insisted. "It's very deep, like the lowest possible bass note of an organ."

"You couldn't hear the shrill whistle when we were coming here," Arthur exclaimed suddenly, "and you can't hear the squeak of a bat. Of course your ears are pitched lower than usual, and you can hear sounds that are lower than I can hear. Listen carefully. Does it sound in the least like a liquid rushing through somewhere?"

"Y-yes," said Estelle hesitatingly. "Somehow, I don't quite understand how, it gives me the impression of a tidal flow or something of that sort."

Arthur rushed indoors. When Estelle followed him she found him excitedly examining the marble floor about the base of the vault.

"It's cracked," he said excitedly. "It's cracked! The vault rose all of an inch!"

Estelle looked and saw the cracks.

"What does that mean?"

"It means we're going to get back where we belong," Arthur cried jubilantly. "It means I'm on the track of the whole trouble. It means everything's going to be all right."

He prowled about the vault exultantly, noting exactly how the cracks in the flooring ran and seeing in each a corroboration of his theory.

"I'll have to make some inspections in the cellar," he went on happily, "but I'm nearly sure I'm on the right track and can figure out a corrective."

"How soon can we hope to start back?" asked Estelle eagerly.

Arthur hesitated, then a great deal of the excitement ebbed from his face, leaving it rather worried and stern.

"It may be a month, or two months, or a year," he answered gravely. "I don't know. If the first thing I try will work, it won't be long. If we have to experiment, I daren't guess how long we may be. But" — his chin set firmly — "we're going to get back."

Estelle looked at him speculatively. Her own expression grew a little worried, too.

"But in a month," she said dubiously, "we — there is hardly any hope of our finding food for two thousand people for a month, is there?"

"We've got to," Arthur declared. "We can't hope to get that much food from the Indians. It will be days before they'll dare to come back to their village, if they ever come. It will be weeks before we can hope to have them earnestly at work to feed us, and that's leaving aside the question of how we'll communicate with them, and how we'll manage to trade with them. Frankly, I think everybody is going to have to draw his belt tight before we get through — if we do. Some of us will get along, anyway."

Estelle's eyes opened wide as the meaning of his last sentence penetrated her mind.

"You mean — that all of us won't —"

"I'm going to take care of you," Arthur said gravely, "but there are liable to be lively doings around here when people begin to realize they're really in a tight fix for food. I'm going to get Van

Deventer to help me organize a police band to enforce martial law. We mustn't have any disorder, that's certain, and I don't trust a city-bred man in a pinch unless I know him."

He stooped and picked up a revolver from the floor, left there by one of the bank watchmen when he fled, in the belief that the building was falling.

VII.

Arthur stood at the window of his office and stared out toward the west. The sun was setting, but upon what a scene!

Where, from this same window Arthur had seen the sun setting behind the Jersey hills, all edged with the angular roofs of factories, with their chimneys emitting columns of smoke, he now saw the same sun sinking redly behind a mass of luxuriant foliage. And where he was accustomed to look upon the tops of high buildings — each entitled to the name of "skyscraper" — he now saw miles and miles of waving green branches.

The wide Hudson flowed on placidly, all unruffled by the arrival of this strange monument upon its shores — the same Hudson Arthur knew as a busy thoroughfare of puffing steamers and chugging launches. Two or three small streams wandered unconcernedly across the land that Arthur had known as the most closely built-up territory on earth. And far, far below him — Arthur had to lean well out of his window to see it — stood a collection of tiny wigwams. Those small bark structures represented the original metropolis of New York.

His telephone rang. Van Deventer was on the wire. The exchange in the building was still working. Van Deventer wanted Arthur to come down to his private office. There were still a great many things to be settled — the arrangements for commandeering offices for sleeping quarters for the women, and numberless other details. The men who seemed to have best kept their heads were gathering there to settle upon a course of action.

Arthur glanced out of the window again before going to the elevator. He saw a curiously compact dark cloud moving swiftly across the sky to the west.

"Miss Woodward," he said sharply, "What is that?"

Estelle came to the window and looked.

"They are birds," she told him. "Birds flying in a group. I've often seen them in the country, though never as many as that."

"How do you catch birds?" Arthur asked her. "I know about

shooting them, and so on, but we haven't guns enough to count. Could we catch them in traps, do you think?"

"I wouldn't be surprised," said Estelle thoughtfully. "But it would be hard to catch many."

"Come downstairs," directed Arthur. "You know as much as any of the men here, and more than most, apparently. We're going to make you show us how to catch things."

Estelle smiled, a trifle wanly. Arthur led the way to the elevator. In the car he noticed that she looked distressed.

"What's the matter?" he asked. "You aren't really frightened, are you?"

"No," she answered shakily, "but — I'm rather upset about this thing. It's so — so terrible, somehow, to be back here, thousands of miles, or years, away from all one's friends and everybody."

"Please" — Arthur smiled encouragingly at her — "please count me your friend, won't you?"

She nodded, but blinked back some tears. Arthur would have tried to hearten her further, but the elevator stopped at their floor. They walked into the room where the meeting of cool heads was to take place.

No more than a dozen men were in there talking earnestly but dispiritedly. When Arthur and Estelle entered Van Deventer came over to greet them.

"We've got to do something," he said in a low voice. "A wave of homesickness has swept over the whole place. Look at those men. Every one is thinking about his family and contrasting his cozy fireside with all that wilderness outside."

"You don't seem to be worried," Arthur observed with a smile.

Van Deventer's eyes twinkled.

"I'm a bachelor," he said cheerfully, "and I live in a hotel. I've been longing for a chance to see some real excitement for thirty years. Business has kept me from it up to now, but I'm enjoying myself hugely."

Estelle looked at the group of dispirited men.

"We'll simply have to do something," she said with a shaky smile. "I feel just as they do. This morning I hated the thought of having to go back to my boarding-house tonight, but right now I feel as if the odor of cabbage in the hallway would seem like heaven."

Arthur led the way to the flat-topped desk in the middle of the room.

"Let's settle a few of the more important matters," he said in a businesslike tone. "None of us has any authority to act for the rest of the people in the tower, but so many of us are in a state of blue funk that those who are here must have charge for a while. Anybody any suggestions?"

"Housing," answered Van Deventer promptly. "I suggest that we draft a gang of men to haul all the upholstered settees and rugs that are to be found to one floor, for the women to sleep on."

"M — m. Yes. That's a good idea. Anybody a better plan?"

No one spoke. They all still looked much too homesick to take any great interest in anything, but they began to listen more or less half heartedly.

"I've been thinking about coal," said Arthur. "There's undoubtedly a supply in the basement, but I wonder if it wouldn't be well to cut the lights off most of the floors, only lighting up the ones we're using."

"That might be a good idea later," Estelle said quietly, "but light is cheering, somehow, and every one feels so blue that I wouldn't do it tonight. Tomorrow they'll begin to get up their resolution again, and you can ask them to do things."

"If we're going to starve to death," one of the other men said gloomily, "we might as well have plenty of light to do it by."

"We aren't going to starve to death," retorted Arthur sharply. "Just before I came down I saw a great cloud of birds, greater than I had ever seen before. When we get at those birds —"

"When," echoed the gloomy one.

"They were pigeons," Estelle explained. "They shouldn't be hard to snare or trap."

"I usually have my dinner before now," the gloomy one protested, "and I'm told I won't get anything tonight."

The other men began to straighten their shoulders. The peevishness of one of their number seemed to bring out their latent courage.

"Well, we've got to stand it for the present," one of them said almost philosophically. "What I'm most anxious about is getting back. Have we any chance?"

Arthur nodded emphatically.

"I think so. I have a sort of idea as to the cause of our sinking into the Fourth Dimension, and when that is verified, a corrective can be looked for and applied."

"How long will that take?"

"Can't say," Arthur replied frankly. "I don't know what tools, what materials, or what workmen we have, and what's rather more to the point, I don't even know what work will have to be done. The pressing problem is food."

"Oh, bother the food," some one protested impatiently. "I don't care about myself. I can go hungry tonight. I want to get back to my family."

"That's all that really matters," a chorus of voices echoed.

"We'd better not bother about anything else unless we find we can't get back. Concentrate on getting back," one man stated more explicitly.

"Look here," said Arthur incisively. "You've a family, and so have a great many of the others in the tower, but your family and everybody else's family has got to wait. As an inside limit, we can hope to begin to work on the problem of getting back when we're sure there's nothing else going to happen. I tell you quite honestly that I think I know what is the direct cause of this catastrophe. And I'll tell you even more honestly that I think I'm the only man among us who can put this tower back where it started from. And I'll tell you most honestly of all that any attempt to meddle at this present time with the forces that let us down here will result in a catastrophe considerably greater than the one that happened today."

"Well, if you're sure —" some one began reluctantly.

"I am so sure that I'm going to keep to myself the knowledge of what will start those forces to work again," Arthur said quietly. "I don't want any impatient meddling. If we start them too soon God only knows what will happen."

VIII.

Van Deventer was eying Arthur Chamberlain keenly.

"It isn't a question of your wanting pay in exchange for your services in putting us back, is it?" he asked coolly.

Arthur turned and faced him. His face began to flush slowly. Van Deventer put up one hand.

"I beg your pardon. I see."

"We aren't settling the things we came here for," Estelle interrupted.

She had noted the threat of friction and hastened to put in a diversion. Arthur relaxed.

"I think that as a beginning," he suggested, "we'd better get sleeping arrangements completed. We can get everybody together somewhere, I dare say, and then secure volunteers for the work."

"Right." Van Deventer was anxious to make amends for his

blunder of a moment before. "Shall I send the bank watchmen to go on each floor in turn and ask everybody to come downstairs?"

"You might start them," Arthur said. "It will take a long time for every one to assemble."

Van Deventer spoke into the telephone on his desk. In a moment he hung up the receiver.

"They're on their way," he said.

Arthur was frowning to himself and scribbling in a notebook.

"Of course," he announced abstractedly, "the pressing problem is food. We've quite a number of fishermen, and a few hunters. We've got to have a lot of food at once, and everything considered, I think we'd better count on the fishermen. At sunrise we'd better have some people begin to dig bait and wake our anglers. They'd better make their tackle tonight, don't you think?"

There was a general nod.

"We'll announce that, then. The fishermen will go to the river under guard of the men we have who can shoot. I think what Indians there are will be much too frightened to try to ambush any of us, but we'd better be on the safe side. They'll keep together and fish at nearly the same spot, with our hunters patrolling the woods behind them, taking potshots at game, if they see any. The fishermen should make more or less of a success, I think. The Indians weren't extensive fishers that I ever heard of, and the river ought fairly to swarm with fish."

He closed his notebook.

"How many weapons can we count on altogether?" Arthur asked Van Deventer.

"In the bank, about a dozen riot-guns and half a dozen repeating rifles. Elsewhere I don't know. Forty or fifty men said they had revolvers, though."

"We'll give revolvers to the men who go with the fishermen. The Indians haven't heard firearms and will run at the report, even if they dare attack our men."

"We can send out the gun-armed men as hunters," some one suggested, "and send gardeners with them to look for vegetables and such things."

"We'll have to take a sort of census, really," Arthur suggested, "finding what every one can do and getting him to do it."

"I never planned anything like this before," Van Deventer remarked, "and I never thought I should, but this is much more fun than running a bank."

Arthur smiled.

"Let's go and have our meeting," he said cheerfully.

But the meeting was a gloomy and despairing affair. Nearly every one had watched the sun set upon a strange, wild landscape. Hardly an individual among the whole two thousand of them had ever been out of sight of a house before in his or her life. To look out at a vast, untouched wilderness where hitherto they had seen the most highly civilized city on the globe would have been startling and depressing enough in itself, but to know that they were alone in a whole continent of savages and that there was not, indeed, in all the world a single community of people they could greet as brothers was terrifying.

Few of them thought so far, but there was actually — if Arthur's estimate of several thousand years' drop back through time was correct — there was actually no other group of English-speaking people in the world. The English language was yet to be invented. Even Rome, the synonym for antiquity of culture, might still be an obscure village inhabited by a band of tatterdemalions under the leadership of an upstart Romulus.

Soft in body as these people were, city-bred and unaccustomed to face other than the most conventionalized emergencies of life, they were terrified. Hardly one of them had even gone without a meal in all his life. To have the prospect of having to earn their food, not by the manipulation of figures in a book, or by expert juggling of profits and prices, but by literal wresting of that food from its source in the earth or stream was a really terrifying thing for them.

In addition, every one of them was bound to the life of modern times by a hundred ties. Many of them had families, a thousand years away. All had interests, engrossing interests, in modern New York.

One young man felt an anxiety that was really ludicrous because he had promised to take his sweetheart to the theater that night, and if he did not come she would be very angry. Another was to have been married in a week. Some of the people were, like Van Deventer and Arthur, so situated that they could view the episode as an adventure, or, like Estelle, who had no immediate fear because all her family was provided for without her help and lived far from New York, so they would not learn of the catastrophe for some time. Many, however, felt instant and pressing fear for the families whose expenses ran always so close to their incomes that the disappearance of the breadwinner for a week would mean actual want or debt. There are very many such families in New York.

The people, therefore, that gathered hopelessly at the call of

Van Deventer's watchmen were dazed and spiritless. Their excitement after Arthur's first attempt to explain the situation to them had evaporated. They were no longer keyed up to a high pitch by the startling thing that had happened to them.

Nevertheless, although only half comprehending what had actually occurred, they began to realize what that occurrence meant. No matter where they might go over the whole face of the globe, they would always be aliens and strangers. If they had been carried away to some unknown shore, some wilderness far from their own land, they might have thought of building ships to return to their homes. They had seen New York vanish before their eyes, however. They had seen their civilization disappear while they watched.

They were in a barbarous world. There was not, for example, a single sulfur match on the whole earth except those in the runaway skyscraper.

IX.

Arthur and Van Deventer, in turn with the others of the cooler heads, thundered at the apathetic people, trying to waken them to the necessity for work. They showered promises of inevitable return to modern times, they pledged their honor to the belief that a way would ultimately be found by which they would all yet find themselves safely back home again.

The people, however, had seen New York disintegrate, and Arthur's explanation sounded like some wild dream of an imaginative novelist. Not one person in all the gathering could actually realize that his home might yet be waiting for him, though at the same time he felt a pathetic anxiety for the welfare of its inmates.

Every one was in a turmoil of contradictory beliefs. On the one hand they knew that all of New York could not be actually destroyed and replaced by a splendid forest in the space of a few hours, so the accident or catastrophe must have occurred to those in the tower, and on the other hand, they had seen all of New York vanish by bits and fragments, to be replaced by a smaller and dingier town, had beheld that replaced in turn, and at last had landed in the midst of this forest.

Every one, too, began to feel an unusual and uncomfortable sensation of hunger. It was a mild discomfort as yet, but few of them had experienced it before without an immediate prospect of assuaging the craving, and the knowledge that there was no food to be had somehow increased the desire for it. They were really in a pitiful state.

Van Deventer spoke encouragingly, and then asked for volunteers for immediate work. There was hardly any response. Every one seemed sunk in despondency. Arthur then began to talk straight from the shoulder and succeeded in rousing them a little, but every one was still rather too frightened to realize that work could help at all.

In desperation the dozen or so men who had gathered in Van Deventer's office went about among the gathering and simply selected men at random, ordering them to follow and begin work. This began to awaken the crowd, but they wakened to fear rather than resolution. They were city-bred, and unaccustomed to face the unusual or the alarming.

Arthur noted the new restlessness, but attributed it to growing uneasiness rather than selfish panic. He was rather pleased that they were outgrowing their apathy. When the meeting had come to an end he felt satisfied that by morning the latent resolution among the people would have crystallized and they would be ready to work earnestly and intelligently on whatever tasks they were directed to undertake.

He returned to the ground floor of the building feeling much more hopeful than before. Two thousand people all earnestly working for one end are hard to down even when faced with such a task as confronted the inhabitants of the runaway skyscraper. Even if they were never able to return to modern times they would still be able to form a community that might do much to hasten the development of civilization in other parts of the world.

His hope received a rude shock when he reached the great hallway on the lower floor. There was a fruit and confectionery stand here, and as Arthur arrived at the spot, he saw a surging mass of men about it. The keeper of the stand looked frightened, but was selling off his stock as fast as he could make change. Arthur forced his way to the counter.

"Here," he said sharply to the keeper of the stand, "stop selling this stuff. It's got to be held until we can dole it out where it's needed."

"I — I can't help myself," the keeper said. "They're takin' it anyway."

"Get back there," Arthur cried to the crowd. "Do you call this decent, trying to get more than your share of this stuff? You'll get your portion tomorrow. It is going to be divided up."

"Go to hell!" some one panted. "You c'n starve if you want to, but I'm goin' to look out f'r myself."

The men were not really starving, but had been put into a panic by the plain speeches of Arthur and his helpers, and were seizing what edibles they could lay hands upon in preparation for the hunger they had been warned to expect.

Arthur pushed against the mob, trying to thrust them away from the counter, but his very effort intensified their panic. There was a quick surge and a crash. The glass front of the showcase broke in.

In a flash of rage Arthur struck out viciously. The crowd paid not the slightest attention to him, however. Every man was too panic-stricken, and too intent on getting some of this food before it was all gone to bother with him.

Arthur was simply crushed back by the bodies of the forty or fifty men. In a moment he found himself alone amid the wreckage of the stand, with the keeper wringing his hands over the remnants of his goods.

Van Deventer ran down the stairs.

"What's the matter?" he demanded as he saw Arthur nursing a bleeding hand cut on the broken glass of the showcase.

"Bolsheviki!" answered Arthur with a grim smile. "We woke up some of the crowd too successfully. They got panic-stricken and started to buy out this stuff here. I tried to stop them, and you see what happened. We'd better look to the restaurant, though I doubt if they'll try anything else just now."

He followed Van Deventer up to the restaurant floor. There were picked men before the door, but just as Arthur and the bank president appeared two or three white-faced men went up to the guards and started low-voiced conversations.

Arthur reached the spot in time to forestall bribery.

Arthur collared one man, Van Deventer another, and in a moment the two were sent reeling down the hallway.

"Some fools have got panic-stricken!" Van Deventer explained to the men before the doors in a casual voice, though he was breathing heavily from the unaccustomed exertion. "They've smashed up the fruit-stand on the ground floor and stolen the contents. It's nothing but blue funk! Only, if any of them start to gather around here, hit them first and talk it over afterward. You'll do that?"

"We will!" the men said heartily.

"Shall we use our guns?" asked another hopefully.

Van Deventer grinned.

"No," he replied, "we haven't any excuse for that yet. But you might shoot at the ceiling, if they get excited. They're just frightened!"

He took Arthur's arm, and the two walked toward the stairway again.

"Chamberlain," he said happily, "tell me why I've never had as much fun as this before!"

Arthur smiled a bit wearily.

"I'm glad you're enjoying yourself!" he said. "I'm not. I'm going outside and walk around. I want to see if any cracks have appeared in the earth anywhere. It's dark, and I'll borrow a lantern down in the fire-room, but I want to find out if there are any more developments in the condition of the building."

X.

Despite his preoccupation with his errand, which was to find if there were other signs of the continued activity of the strange forces that had lowered the tower through the Fourth Dimension into the dim and unrecorded years of aboriginal America, Arthur could not escape the fascination of the sight that met his eyes. A bright moon shone overhead and silvered the white sides of the tower, while the brightly lighted windows of the offices within glittered like jewels set into the shining shaft.

From his position on the ground he looked into the dimness of the forest on all sides. Black obscurity had gathered beneath the dark masses of moonlit foliage. The tiny birch-bark teepees of the now deserted Indian village glowed palely. Above, the stars looked calmly down at the accusing finger of the tower pointing upward, as if in reproach at their indifference to the savagery that reigned over the whole earth.

Like a fairy tower of jewels the building rose. Alone among a wilderness of trees and streams it towered in a strange beauty: moonlit to silver, lighted from within to a mass of brilliant gems, it stood serenely still.

Arthur, carrying his futile lantern about its base, felt his own insignificance as never before. He wondered what the Indians must think. He knew there must be hundreds of eyes fixed upon the strange sight — fixed in awe-stricken terror or superstitious reverence upon this unearthly visitor to their hunting grounds.

A tiny figure, dwarfed by the building whose base he skirted,

Arthur moved slowly about the vast pile. The earth seemed not to have been affected by the vast weight of the tower.

Arthur knew, however, that long concrete piles reached far down to bedrock. It was these piles that had sunk into the Fourth Dimension, carrying the building with them.

Arthur had followed the plans with great interest when the Metropolitan was constructed. It was an engineering feat, and in the engineering periodicals, whose study was a part of Arthur's business, great space had been given to the building and the methods of its construction.

While examining the earth carefully he went over his theory of the cause for the catastrophe. The whole structure must have sunk at the same time, or it, too, would have disintegrated, as the other buildings had appeared to disintegrate. Mentally, Arthur likened the submergence of the tower in the oceans of time to an elevator sinking past the different floors of an office building. All about the building the other skyscrapers of New York had seemed to vanish. In an elevator, the floors one passes seem to rise upward.

Carrying out the analogy to its logical end, Arthur reasoned that the building itself had no more cause to disintegrate, as the buildings it passed seemed to disintegrate, than the elevator in the office building would have cause to rise because its surroundings seemed to rise.

Within the building, he knew, there were strange stirrings of emotions. Queer currents of panic were running about, throwing the people to and fro as leaves are thrown about by a current of wind. Yet, underneath all those undercurrents of fear, was a rapidly growing resolution, strengthened by an increasing knowledge of the need to work.

Men were busy even then shifting all possible comfortable furniture to a single story for the women in the building to occupy. The men would sleep on the floor for the present. Beds of boughs could be improvised on the morrow. At sunrise on the following morning many men would go to the streams to fish, guarded by other men. All would be frightened, no doubt, but there would be a grim resolution underneath the fear. Other men would wander about to hunt.

There was little likelihood of Indians approaching for some days, at least, but when they did come Arthur meant to avoid hostilities by all possible means. The Indians would be fearful of their strange visitors, and it should not be difficult to convince them that friendliness was safest, even if they displayed unfriendly desires.

The pressing problem was food. There were two thousand people in the building, soft-bodied and city-bred. They were unaccustomed to hardship, and could not endure what more primitive people would hardly have noticed.

They must be fed, but first they must be taught to feed themselves. The fishermen would help, but Arthur could only hope that they would prove equal to the occasion. He did not know what to expect from them. From the hunters he expected but little. The Indians were wary hunters, and game would be shy if not scarce.

The great cloud of birds he had seen at sunset was a hopeful sign. Arthur vaguely remembered stories of great flocks of wood-pigeons which had been exterminated, as the buffalo was exterminated. As he considered the remembrance became more clear.

They had flown in huge flocks which nearly darkened the sky. As late as the forties of the nineteenth century they had been an important article of food, and had glutted the market at certain seasons of the year.

Estelle had said the birds he had seen at sunset were pigeons. Perhaps this was one of the great flocks. If it were really so, the food problem would be much lessened, provided a way could be found to secure them. The ammunition in the tower was very limited, and a shell could not be found for every bird that was needed, nor even for every three or four. Great traps must be devised, or bird-lime might possibly be produced. Arthur made a mental note to ask Estelle if she knew anything of bird-lime.

A vague, humming roar, altering in pitch, came to his ears. He listened for some time before he identified it as the sound of the wind playing upon the irregular surfaces of the tower. In the city the sound was drowned by the multitude of other noises, but here Arthur could hear it plainly.

He listened a moment, and became surprised at the number of night noises he could hear. In New York he had closed his ears to incidental sounds from sheer self-protection. Somewhere he heard the ripple of a little spring. As the idea of a spring came into his mind, he remembered Estelle's description of the deep-toned roar she had heard.

He put his hand on the cold stone of the building. There was still a vibrant quivering of the rock. It was weaker than before, but was still noticeable.

He drew back from the rock and looked up into the sky. It seemed to blaze with stars, far more stars than Arthur had ever seen in the city, and more than he had dreamed existed.

As he looked, however, a cloud seemed to film a portion of the heavens. The stars still showed through it, but they twinkled in a peculiar fashion that Arthur could not understand.

He watched in growing perplexity. The cloud moved very swiftly. Thin as it seemed to be, it should have been silvery from the moonlight, but the sky was noticeably darker where it moved. It advanced toward the tower and seemed to obscure the upper portion. A confused motion became visible among its parts. Wisps of it whirled away from the brilliantly lighted tower, and then returned swiftly toward it.

Arthur heard a faint tinkle, then a musical scraping, which became louder. A faint scream sounded, then another. The tinkle developed into the sound made by breaking glass, and the scraping sound became that of the broken fragments as they rubbed against the sides of the tower in their fall.

The scream came again. It was the frightened cry of a woman. A soft body struck the earth not ten feet from where Arthur stood, then another, and another.

XI.

Arthur urged the elevator boy to greater speed. They were speeding up the shaft as rapidly as possible, but it was not fast enough. When they at last reached the height at which the excitement seemed to be centered, the car was stopped with a jerk and Arthur dashed down the hall.

Half a dozen frightened stenographers stood there, huddled together.

"What's the matter?" Arthur demanded. Men were running from the other floors to see what the trouble was.

"The — the windows broke, and — and something flew in at us!" one of them gasped. There was a crash inside the nearest office and the women screamed again.

Arthur drew a revolver from his pocket and advanced to the door. He quickly threw it open, entered, and closed it behind him. Those left out in the hall waited tensely.

There was no sound. The women began to look even more frightened. The men shuffled their feet uneasily, and looked uncomfortably at one another. Van Deventer appeared on the scene, puffing a little from his haste.

The door opened again and Arthur came out. He was carrying something in his hands. He had put his revolver aside and looked somewhat foolish but very much delighted.

"The food question is settled," he said happily. "Look!"

He held out the object he carried. It was a bird, apparently a pigeon of some sort. It seemed to have been stunned, but as Arthur held it out it stirred, then struggled, and in a moment was flapping wildly in an attempt to escape.

"It's a wood-pigeon," said Arthur. "They must fly after dark sometimes. A big flock of them ran afoul of the tower and were dazed by the lights. They've broken a lot of windows, I dare say, but a great many of them ran into the stonework and were stunned. I was outside the tower, and when I came in they were dropping to the ground by hundreds. I didn't know what they were then, but if we wait twenty minutes or so I think we can go out and gather up our supper and breakfast and several other meals, all at once."

Estelle had appeared and now reached out her hands for the bird.

"I'll take care of this one," she said. "Wouldn't it be a good idea to see if there aren't some more stunned in the other offices?"

In half an hour the electric stoves of the restaurant were going at their full capacity. Men, cheerfully excited men now, were bringing in pigeons by armfuls, and other men were skinning them. There was no time to pluck them, though a great many of the women were busily engaged in that occupation.

As fast as the birds could be cooked they were served out to the impatient but much cheered castaways, and in a little while nearly every person in the place was walking casually about the halls with a roasted, broiled, or fried pigeon in his hands. The ovens were roasting pigeons, the frying pans were frying them, and the broilers were loaded down with the small but tender birds.

The unexpected solution of the most pressing question cheered every one amazingly. Many people were still frightened, but less frightened than before. Worry for their families still oppressed a great many, but the removal of the fear of immediate hunger led them to believe that the other problems before them would be solved, too, and in as satisfactory a manner.

Arthur had returned to his office with four broiled pigeons in a sheet of wrapping paper. As he somehow expected, Estelle was waiting there.

"Thought I'd bring lunch up," he announced. "Are you hungry?"

"Starving!" Estelle replied, and laughed.

The whole catastrophe began to become an adventure. She bit eagerly into a bird. Arthur began as hungrily on another. For some time neither spoke a word. At last, however, Arthur waved the leg of his second pigeon toward his desk.

"Look what we've got here!" he said.

Estelle nodded. The stunned pigeon Arthur had first picked up was tied by one foot to a paperweight.

"I thought we might keep him for a souvenir," she suggested.

"You seem pretty confident we'll get back, all right," Arthur observed. "It was surely lucky those blessed birds came along. They've heartened up the people wonderfully!"

"Oh, I knew you'd manage somehow!" said Estelle confidently.

"I manage?" Arthur repeated, smiling. "What have I done?"

"Why, you've done everything," affirmed Estelle stoutly. "You've told the people what to do from the very first, and you're going to get us back."

Arthur grinned, then suddenly his face grew a little more serious.

"I wish I were as sure as you are," he said. "I think we'll be all right, though, sooner or later."

"I'm sure of it," Estelle declared with conviction. "Why, you — "

"Why I?" asked Arthur again. He bent forward in his chair and fixed his eyes on Estelle's. She looked up, met his gaze, and stammered.

"You — you do things," she finished lamely.

"I'm tempted to do something now," Arthur said. "Look here, Miss Woodward, you've been in my employ for three or four months. In all that time I've never had anything but the most impersonal comments from you. Why the sudden change?"

The twinkle in his eyes robbed his words of any impertinence.

"Why, I really — I really suppose I never noticed you before," said Estelle.

"Please notice me hereafter," said Arthur. "I have been noticing you. I've been doing practically nothing else."

Estelle flushed again. She tried to meet Arthur's eyes and failed. She bit desperately into her pigeon drumstick, trying to think of something to say.

"When we get back," went on Arthur meditatively, "I'll have nothing to do — no work or anything. I'll be broke and out of a job."

Estelle shook her head emphatically. Arthur paid no attention.

"Estelle," he said, smiling, "would you like to be out of a job with me?"

Estelle turned crimson.

"I'm not very successful," Arthur went on soberly. "I'm afraid I wouldn't make a very good husband, I'm rather worthless and lazy!"

"You aren't," broke in Estelle; "you're — you're —"

Arthur reached over and took her by the shoulders.

"What?" he demanded.

She would not look at him, but she did not draw away. He held her from him for a moment.

"What am I?" he demanded again. Somehow he found himself kissing the tips of her ears. Her face was buried against his shoulder.

"What am I?" he repeated sternly.

Her voice was muffled by his coat.

"You're — you're dear!" she said.

There was an interlude of about a minute and a half, then she pushed him away from her.

"Don't!" she said breathlessly. "Please don't!"

"Aren't you going to marry me?" he demanded.

Still crimson, she nodded shyly. He kissed her again.

"Please don't!" she protested.

She fondled the lapels of his coat, quite content to have his arms about her.

"Why mayn't I kiss you if you're going to marry me?" Arthur demanded.

She looked up at him with an air of demure primness.

"You — you've been eating pigeon," she told him in mock gravity, "and   and your mouth is greasy!"

XII.

It was two weeks later. Estelle looked out over the now familiar wild landscape. It was much the same when she looked far away, but near by there were great changes.

A cleared trail led through the woods to the waterfront, and a raft of logs extended out into the river for hundreds of feet. Both sides of the raft were lined with busy fishermen — men and women, too. A little to the north of the base of the building a huge mound of earth smoked sullenly. The coal in the cellar had given out and charcoal had been found to be the best substitute they could improvise. The mound was where the charcoal was made.

It was heartbreaking work to keep the fires going with charcoal, because it burned so rapidly in the powerful draft of the furnaces, but the original fire-room gang had been recruited to several times its original number from among the towerites, and the work was divided until it did not seem hard.

As Estelle looked down two tiny figures sauntered across the clearing from the woods with a heavy animal slung between them. One of them was using a gun as a walking-stick. Estelle saw the flash of the sun on its polished metal barrel.

There were a number of Indians in the clearing, watching with wide-open eyes the activities of the whites. Dozens of birch-bark canoes dotted the Hudson, each with its load of fishermen, industriously working for the white people. It had been hard to overcome the fear in the Indians, and they still paid superstitious reverence to the whites, but fair dealings, coupled with a constant readiness to defend themselves, had enabled Arthur to institute a system of trading for food that had so far proved satisfactory.

The whites had found spare lightbulbs valuable currency in dealing with the redmen. Picture-wire, too, was highly prized. There was not a picture left hanging in any of the offices. Metal paper-knives bought huge quantities of provisions from the eager Indian traders, and the story was current in the tower that Arthur had received eight canoe-loads of corn and vegetables in exchange for a broken-down typewriter. No one could guess what the savages wanted with the typewriter, but they had carted it away triumphantly.

Estelle smiled tenderly to herself as she remembered how Arthur had been the leading spirit in all the numberless enterprises in which the castaways had been forced to engage. He would come to her in a spare ten minutes, and tell her how everything was going. He seemed curiously boylike in those moments.

Sometimes he would come straight from the fire-room — he insisted on taking part in all the more arduous duties — having hastily cleaned himself for her inspection, snatch a hurried kiss, and then go off, laughing, to help chop down trees for the long fishing-raft. He had told them how to make charcoal, had taken a leading part in establishing and maintaining friendly relations with the Indians, and was now down in the deepest sub-basement, working with a gang of volunteers to try to put the building back where it belonged.

Estelle had said, after the collapse of the flooring in the board-room, that she heard a sound like the rushing of waters. Arthur, on examining the floor where the safe-deposit vault stood, found it had risen an inch. On these facts he had built up his theory. The building, like all modern skyscrapers, rested on concrete piles extending down to bedrock. In the center of one of those piles there was a hollow tube originally intended to serve as an artesian well. The flow had been insufficient and the well had been stopped up.

Arthur, of course, as an engineer, had studied the construc-tion of the building with great care, and happened to remember that this partly hollow pile was the one nearest the safe-deposit vault. The collapse of the board-room floor had suggested that some change had happened in the building itself, and that was found when he saw that the deposit-vault had actually risen an inch.

He at once connected the rise in the flooring above the hollow pile with the pipe in the pile. Estelle had heard liquid sounds. Evi-dently water had been forced into the hollow artesian pipe under an unthinkable pressure when the catastrophe occurred.

From the rumbling and the suddenness of the whole catas-trophe a volcanic or seismic disturbance was evident. The con-nection of volcanic or seismic action with a flow of water sug-gested a geyser or a hot spring of some sort, probably a spring which had broken through its normal confines some time be-fore, but whose pressure had been sufficient to prevent the acci-dent until the failure of its flow.

When the flow ceased the building sank rapidly. For the fact that this "sinking" was in the fourth direction — the Fourth Dimension — Arthur had no explanation. He simply knew that in some mysterious way an outlet for the pressure had developed in that fashion, and that the tower had followed the spring in its fall through time.

The sole apparent change in the building had occurred above the one hollow concrete pile, which seemed to indicate that if access were to be had to the mysterious, and so far only assumed spring, it must be through that pile. While the vault retained its abnormal elevation, Arthur believed that there was still water at an immense and incalculable pressure in the pipe. He dared not attempt to tap the pipe until the pressure had abated.

At the end of a week he found the vault slowly settling back into place. When its return to the normal was complete he dared begin boring a hole to reach the hollow tube in the concrete pile.

As he suspected, he found water in the pile — water whose sulfurous and mineral nature confirmed his belief that a geyser reaching deep into the bosom of the earth, as well as far back in the realms of time, was at the bottom of the extraordinary jaunt of the tower.

Geysers were still far from satisfactory things to explain. There are many of their vagaries which we cannot understand at all. We do know a few things which affect them, and one thing is that "soaping" them will stimulate their flow in an extraordinary manner.

Arthur proposed to "soap" this mysterious geyser when the renewal of its flow should lift the runaway skyscraper back to the epoch from which the failure of the flow had caused it to fall.

He made his preparations with great care. He confidently expected his plan to work, and to see the skyscraper once more towering over midtown New York as was its wont, but he did not allow the fishermen and hunters to relax their efforts on that account. They labored as before, while deep down in the sub-basement of the colossal building Arthur and his volunteers toiled mightily.

They had to bore through the concrete pile until they reached the hollow within it. Then, when the evidence gained from the water in the pipe had confirmed his surmises, they had to prepare their "charge" of soapy liquids by which the geyser was to be stirred to renewed activity.

Great quantities of the soap used by the scrubwomen in scrubbing down the floors was boiled with water until a sirupy mess was evolved. Means had then to be provided by which this could be quickly introduced into the hollow pile, the hole then closed, and then braced to withstand a pressure unparalleled in hydraulic science. Arthur believed that from the hollow pile the soapy liquid would find its way to the geyser proper, where it would take effect in stimulating the lessened flow to its former proportions. When that took place he believed that the building would return as swiftly and as surely as it had left them to normal, modern times.

The telephone rang in his office, and Estelle answered it. Arthur was on the wire. A signal was being hung out for all the castaway to return to the building from their several occupations. They were about to soap the geyser.

Did Estelle want to come down and watch? She did! She stood in the main hallway as the excited and hopeful people trooped in. When the last was inside the doors were firmly closed. The few friendly Indians outside stared perplexedly at the mysterious white strangers.

The whites, laughing excitedly, began to wave to the Indians. Their leave-taking was premature.

Estelle took her way down into the cellar. Arthur was awaiting her arrival. Van Deventer stood near, with the grinning, grimy members of Arthur's volunteer work gang. The massive concrete pile stood in the center of the cellar. A big steam-boiler was coupled to a tiny pipe that led into the heart of the mass of concrete. Arthur was going to force the soapy liquid into the hollow pile by steam.

At a signal steam began to hiss in the boiler. Live steam from the fire-room forced the soapy sirup out of the boiler, through the small iron pipe, into the hollow that led to the geyser far underground. Six thousand gallons in all were forced into the opening in a space of three minutes.

Arthur's grimy gang began to work with desperate haste. Quickly they withdrew the iron pipe and inserted a long steel plug, painfully beaten from a bar of solid metal. Then, girding the colossal concrete pile, ring after ring of metal was slipped on, to hold the plug in place.

The last of the safeguards was hardly fastened firmly when Estelle listened intently.

"I hear a rumbling!" she said quietly.

Arthur reached forward and put his hand on the mass of concrete.

"It is quivering!" he reported as quietly. "I think we'll be on our way in a very little while."

The group broke for the stairs, to watch the panorama as the runaway skyscraper made its way back through the thousands of years to the times that had built it for a monument to modern commerce.

Arthur and Estelle went high up in the tower. From the window of Arthur's office they looked eagerly, and felt the slight quiver as the tower got under way. Estelle looked up at the sun, and saw it mend its pace toward the west.

Night fell.

The evening sounds became high-pitched and shrill, then seemed to cease altogether.

In a very little while there was light again, and the sun was speeding across the sky. It sank hastily, and returned almost immediately, *via* the east. Its pace became a breakneck rush. Down behind the hills and up in the east. Down in the west, up in the east. Down and up — The flickering began. The race back toward modern times had started.

Arthur and Estelle stood at the window and looked out as the sun rushed more and more rapidly across the sky until it became but a streak of light, shifting first to the right and then to the left as the seasons passed in their turn.

With Arthur's arms about her shoulders, Estelle stared out across the unbelievable landscape, while the nights and days, the winters and summers, and the storms and calms of a thousand years swept past them into the irrevocable past.

Presently Arthur drew her to him and kissed her. While he kissed her, so swiftly did the days and years flee by, three generations were born, grew and begot children, and died again!

Estelle, held fast in Arthur's arms, thought nothing of such trivial things. She put her arms about his neck and kissed him, while the years passed them unheeded.

Of course you know that the building landed safely, in the exact hour, minute, and second from which it started, so that when the frightened and excited people poured out of it to stand in Madison Square and feel that the world was once more right side up, their hilarious and incomprehensible conduct made such of the world as was passing by think a contagious madness had broken out.

Days passed before the story of the two thousand was believed, but at last it was accepted as truth, and eminent scientists studied the matter exhaustively.

There has been one rather queer result of the journey of the runaway skyscraper. A certain Isidore Eckstein, a dealer in jewelry novelties, whose office was in the tower when it disappeared into the past, has entered suit in the courts of the United States against all the holders of land on Manhattan Island. It seems that during the two weeks in which the tower rested in the wilderness he traded independently with one of the Indian chiefs, and in exchange for two near-pearl necklaces, sixteen finger-rings, and one dollar in money, received a title-deed to the entire island. — He claims that his deed is a conveyance made previous to all other sales whatever.

Strictly speaking, he is undoubtedly right, as his deed was signed before the discovery of America. The courts, however, are deliberating the question with a great deal of perplexity.

Eckstein is quite confident that in the end his claim will be allowed and he will be admitted as the sole owner of real-estate on

Manhattan Island, with all occupiers of buildings and territory paying him ground rent at a rate he will fix himself. In the mean time, though the foundations are being reinforced so the catastrophe cannot occur again, his entire office is packed full of articles suitable for trading with the Indians. If the tower makes another trip back through time, Eckstein hopes to become a landholder of some importance.

No less than eighty-seven books have been written by members of the memorable two thousand in description of their trip to the hinterland of time, but Arthur, who could write more intelligently about the matter than any one else, is so extremely busy that he cannot bother with such things. He has two very important matters to look after. One is, of course, the reenforcement of the foundations of the building so that a repetition of the catastrophe cannot occur, and the other is to convince his wife — who is Estelle, naturally — that she is the most adorable person in the universe. He finds the latter task the more difficult, because she insists that *he* is the most adorable person —

THE GALLERY GODS

The white-painted fruit steamer steamed out between the forts and turned toward the south. She only touched at Bahia del Toro to drop the mail on her downward trip, though on her return toward the north she paused to take on a portion of her cargo. The Stars and Stripes at her masthead fluttered brightly in the golden sunshine of midday, and the same sunshine made the sea seem bluer, and the palms greener and vividly alive. Half a dozen small launches that had clustered about the white ship scattered and made for different points along the waterfront of the city.

El Señor Beckwith was seated in a great cane chair on the veranda of the white house that sprawled over the hillside. He looked at the ship and heaved a sigh. It was not a wistful sigh, nor was there pathos concealed anywhere about it. The sigh was a sign of the satisfaction that filled him. He sat at ease, puffing a long black cigar. At his elbow a glass tinkled musically when he moved. His huge frame, now clad in spotless white duck, was eloquent of content. Only his left thumb, bandaged and in splints, gave the slightest sign of discomfort, and he smiled when he felt the encumbrance of the wrappings. It was a souvenir of the incident that caused his sensation of complete satisfaction. Conway had broken that thumb in his last struggle, two weeks before, in New York. Conway was dead.

There was a clattering of tiny hoofs. One of the houseboys had been down to the wharf to get the New York papers Beckwith had arranged should be sent him. They would contain the details of Conway's death, and Beckwith drew in a pleasurable breath at the thought of reading them.

The little donkey had brought the boy hastily up with his light burden, and now the brown-skinned boy came in to Beckwith, The papers were all there, with all their "magazine sections," their "rotogravure" illustrations, and all the other minor features on which they prided themselves. As the newspapers were handed to him, Beckwith even noticed a gaudily colored comic section. He flicked it carelessly aside.

These flimsy bundles of print had been brought four thousand miles for him to enjoy this moment. He would read of the death of Hugh Conway, multimillionaire philanthropist, patron of the arts, and other worthy things to the extent of a reportorial vocabulary, killed in the most open and daring fashion by William Beckwith, now at large. He would read of the letter left pinned to the multimillionaire's breast in which that same William Beckwith announced his reasons for killing the millionaire, and the precise fashion in which he intended to escape punishment.

Beckwith smiled cheerfully to himself as he visualized in advance the excited indignation with which the editorial comment would point out the loophole of which he had taken advantage. For weeks to come there would be indignation and anger at his calm defiance of the law and the power of the United States, while here in Bahia del Toro he would live openly and happily, frankly glorifying in the crime he had committed, respected and feared by the people.

There were the newspapers. The murder of Hugh Conway would be good for a scare-head on the front page.

Beckwith spread out the paper with his uninjured hand and ran his eye over the headlines. Hugh Conway — Hugh Conway. Where was it? Not on the first page. Beckwith glanced at the date with a frown. The date was that of the day after the murder, and surely it should have been a news feature. He looked on the second page. Nothing there: He ran his eye over the third page and the fourth.

He flung the flimsy sheet impatiently aside and picked a second. The date was the same, and the name of the paper was that of one of the most sensational journals in New York. That, at least, would play up the murder in great shape. A new airplane record, a crisis in Europe, a prominent divorce case. Not *one* word of Hugh Conway. The second page.

Beckwith rumpled the newspaper and threw it away. He bit angrily on his cigar. He had killed Conway, strangled him with his two hands. He took up the third paper, then the fourth. Not a word concerning Conway. Beckwith growled throatily, then an idea struck him.

The police might have concealed the crime for a day or more, hoping to ensnare him before he escaped. A later paper would tell. Beckwith's brow cleared. Of course that was it. He half smiled as he realized how typical such an action would be. The police would want to announce the crime and the arrest of the murderer at the same time. Wells, the commissioner of police, was fond of just such tricks. He and Beckwith and Conway had gone to school together, and Beckwith knew Wells down to the ground.

With a leisurely gesture he selected a newspaper of the day following, and unfolded it, only to frown again. The first page was still devoted to commonplace events, and the second likewise. Still another one was barren of news on the topic that was all-important to Beckwith. He impatiently cast them down and examined those of the next day, and the next. When the last of his newspapers had joined the crumpled pile at his feet, Beckwith sat helplessly puzzled.

He was both puzzled and annoyed. His left thumb was bandaged, where Conway had dislocated it in his struggle for life. The cumbrous wrapping was still reminder of that event. Conway was dead, had been dead for three weeks, but for at least one week after his death no mention of him had appeared in any New York newspaper.

Why? Conway was well known and an important figure in the financial world. His murder, surely, would be a news item of the first importance. But not one single paragraph had been devoted to him. Beckwith had strangled him in his own motorcar, then knocked the chauffeur unconscious and escaped to a waiting yacht. The mere melodrama of the feat was enough to make it "copy" for the whole United States, let alone the city of New York. But every newspaper in New York had ignored it, as they had ignored Beckwith's scornful letter, sarcastically giving his address to the police.

Dusk had faded into twilight, and twilight into diamond-studded night. Down in the city the band played faintly in the plaza, while the long lines of dark-eyed *señoritas* promenaded primly in a duenna-guarded circle, listening decorously to the music, but casting liquid glances at the olive-skinned young men who less primly strolled in the other direction, twirling their budding mustaches for the admiration of the fairer sex. Now and again the muted chords of a guitar tinkled through the air, and now and again bursts of more uproariously amorous festivity came from the section of the town devoted to the *cantinas* and their less frank adjuncts.

Beckwith put his hat upon his head and sallied into the cobble-stoned street. He would go to the American Club. Soon, he was grimly aware, he would be barred from its precincts, unless his importance under the Garrios government overcame the normal dislike of the Anglo-Saxon for a murderer. He would go there tonight in any event. The newspapers might not have printed details of Conway's murder, but Melton, the American consul, would surely have been cabled.

Beckwith had told in his sarcastic note to Wells that he would make for Bahia del Toro, and Wells would certainly wire the consulate to find if he had actually appeared. Beckwith grinned as he thought of the touching faith of the civilian American in the efficacy of a demand by a consular representative. Wells would insist that the Nueva Bolivian government turn the criminal over to justice. He would ignore the absence of a treaty of extradition.

The interior of the club was painfully hot, and most of the members sat upon the terrace above the entrance, sipping drinks from glasses that tinkled musically. Two or three cigars glowed fitfully in the obscurity, and the white-clad figure of the *mozo* moving from chair to chair was wraithlike.

Beckwith stood in the doorway a moment before entering. The band was good, even for a military band among a musical people. At the moment it was playing a soft and dreamy waltz, while the young people in the plaza below eddied in their endless circles, the women inside, prim and decorous, and the men without, discreetly admiring. Half a dozen sputtering lights detracted from the romance of the scene, but made it possible to catch an occasional glimpse of some darkly beautiful face, outlined in the sharp glow of the arc-lamp.

Beckwith paid no attention to that phase of the scene, but searched among the seated, coatless figures for Melton the consul. Melton had drawn his chair close to the railing and was looking out and down upon the plaza with a wistful expression. Beckwith caught sight of him when the glow of his cigar lighted up his face for a moment. With an assumption of indifference, Beckwith dropped into the chair by his side. Melton turned and squinted at him through the darkness until he recognized who it was.

"Oh, hello, Beckwith," he said casually. "Hot, isn't it?"

He turned and surveyed the prim crowd below him, without waiting for Beckwith's acknowledgment. Melton was silent for a moment or so.

"Beckwith," he said presently, "do you know what this reminds me of? It reminds me of Springfield, Massachusetts, about November. It's so different." He half smiled to himself in the darkness. "I remember I used to be going about this time to call on some girl, with a box of candy under my arm."

"*Mozo*," said Beckwith harshly. The boy came and took his order.

"You've been down here ten years," went on the consul, still in that half-hushed tone of reminiscence, "I've been away five years from the States, but I can still picture it. Crowds of people going into vaudeville houses, others climbing excitedly on streetcars. I'd give a lot to have a street-car clang a bell at me just about now."

"I was in New York two weeks ago," said Beckwith suddenly, half minded to blurt out his reason for going north and what he had done there. "Went up there, but it was all strange. I wasn't comfortable until I got back here."

"I hope I won't feel strange," said the consul dreamily. "I'm going back next year. Do you know, I'm thinking about fried fish. They don't have the same kinds of fish down here, and they don't cook them the same way. The first thing I'm going to do when I land in New York, is to eat a meal in a restaurant. And I'm going to have fried fish and griddlecakes with maple syrup. I don't know why fried fish appeals to me so much," he added thoughtfully, "because I never cared much for them when I could get them."

Beckwith moved uneasily.

"Any news lately?" he asked, succeeding very well in keeping his tone casual.

"Nothing but the papers," answered Melton abstractedly. "Your boy was down at the dock and got a batch of them. I say, Beckwith —"

He launched forth in a vivid description of the joys of living in Springfield, Massachusetts, to which Beckwith listened uninterestedly, but perforce, sipping at his grenadine Rickey from time to time. When he left, Beckwith was puzzled, but convinced that there had been no message or inquiry sent to Melton from the States concerning him.

He went slowly up to his white house that sprawled over the hillside, wondering why. As he was entering his own door the obvious solution came to him.

Wells would naturally have tried to keep the murder secret for twenty-four hours. That was one of his favorite tricks, keeping a crime secret to afford himself so much start in his efforts to unravel the mystery, so that the story of the crime and the capture of the criminal could be announced at the same time. Twenty-four hours was usually his limit. Evidently, however, he had been able to extend the time on this occasion. He must have possessed an incredible influence with the newspapers to keep them for seven days from exploiting so succulent a morsel of melodrama.

Beckwith chuckled. Wells was trying to save his face. He had held off public knowledge of his failure for a week, but would be unable to keep it up much longer. When the next mail came, in seven days more, the newspapers would spread the news of Conway's death and Wells's humiliation, with Beckwith's triumph as their principal theme. A man who so defiantly flouted the law, who sneered at the police to the extent of giving them his address, would surely be made much of by the press, even if they denounced him. The next mail would tell the story, and Wells's humiliation would be the more complete for being delayed. The newspapers would flay him for trying to conceal the crime.

Beckwith went to sleep with a sense of profound satisfaction in spite of his recent disappointment.

The steamer usually made the port of Bahia del Toro about noon, but as early as nine o'clock in the morning of the next steamer day Beckwith was looking down the coastline for the smudge of smoke that would portend the arrival of the vessel. He swept the horizon with his glasses from time to time, growing more and more impatient. The white hull did not appear until nearly four, however, and it was five o'clock before it turned in between the forts. Beckwith went out in one of the launches to meet it, smiling in anticipation of triumph. He waved gaily to the globetrotting passengers clustered by the after rail. They would know of Conway's death, and one of the officers of the ship would undoubtedly point him out as the man who had defied the law.

The bundle of newspapers fell into the launch with a heavy thump, and the purser who had dropped them over waved a friendly hand. The little boat backed off from the steamer and sped toward the shore, while Beckwith cut the twine about his package of papers and began to run rapidly through them, glancing only at the first-page headlines.

The first, no, the second, no, the third. A curious sensation settled upon him. Bewilderment and unreasoning suspicion, then poignant disappointment, finally a persistent hope. He could not examine them all thoroughly in the launch. The wind threatened to blow them overboard, but he put them together in a compact package and waited impatiently until he could go over them in detail at his home. He hastened to his house, carrying the parcel himself. He hurried into his smoking-room and flung them on the table, then went over them again, and again, each time more minutely, each time with growing incredulity.

Not one newspaper issued on any day of the second week after the murder of Hugh Conway contained one hint of that event. Not one word, line, or paragraph referred to the murder of Hugh Conway by William Beckwith. Not one faintest indication appeared in any issue of any periodical during the second week after that murder of the defiant note written by the murderer to the commissioner of police. There was nothing to make any one suspect that any harm had come to one of the foremost figures in American finance.

Beckwith rubbed his forehead in amazement and perplexity. His dislocated thumb was still tender where Conway had struggled to save his life. His memory of the event was lucid and complete. He *knew* that he had killed Conway.

During the following week he brooded almost continuously over his problem. He cabled a confidential message to the Nueva Bolivian consul in New York, who knew his influence with Garrios well enough to heed his requests, asking for information about Conway. The consulate replied with a succinct list of his offices as head of this and that corporation, and added that his present whereabouts were unknown.

The message cheered Beckwith immensely. He made a resolution to wait one more week. If there was still no public news of Conway's death, he would write to the New York papers and put them in possession of the facts. He, William Beckwith, had killed Conway with his bare hands, and now resided openly in the city of Bahia del Toro. He would defy the police to punish him, and expose the duplicity of the commissioner of police, who had concealed the crime for no less than two weeks.

The steamer date arrived, but Beckwith was no longer impatient. He was calmly confident that there would be no mention of the crime in the newspapers of this week. Wells might prevent the news from even becoming public. Beckwith had been so long in the Latin countries, where censorship is ruthless and complete, that he did not realize the impracticability of such a plan.

He watched the steamer arrive and drop the mailbags over the side without emotion other than an abstract interest. When she came back on her way north again, he would have letters to form a part of her cargo; letters which would upset the smug complacency of the city of New York. A sodden, heavy rain was falling when the steamer made port, and it was barely visible from the house on the hill because of the sheets of falling water. Beckwith stood for a moment on his veranda and strained his eyes through the misty obscurity. The grass was exhaling fresh and fragrant odors in the rainfall. The palm leaves were dark and glistening with the wet. Outside, the cobblestones of the street were running miniature floods of water to the gutter, Beckwith sat comfortably indoors and smoked one of his thin black cigars, quite tranquil, waiting for the boy to bring him the papers for which he had sent.

Presently, above the humming roar of the rain on the roof and street, he heard the donkey's hoofs. A door opened. A boy's voice spoke in liquid Spanish, and then one of the servants brought him a rain-sodden bundle of flimsy printed sheets. Beckwith quite calmly cut the twine. The papers on the inside were dry, and he spread one out, looking at it with interest which sought confirmation of a conclusion already made. Wells had concealed the crime.

"Hugh Conway —" The name leaped at him from the head-lines. A shock went over Beckwith so that for a moment he could read no more. His hands were shaking. Triumph welled up in his heart. He laughed for an instant, and steadied his hands against the table before him. He fixed his eyes on the printed page.

A moment later his always-frightened half-caste wife was shrinking in terror from the room she had been about to enter. Her husband was in there, staring at a sheet of paper and pouring out imprecations from the dregs of two languages. He seemed so furious that his anger verged on panic.

"Hugh Conway Announces Gift to City's Poor!" The headlines were those of the "feature section" of one of the larger newspapers which invariably made much of the benevolences of the rich. Below the headline a pen-and-ink portrait of Hugh Conway — Hugh Conway, whom Beckwith had killed a month before — smiled from the page.

Beckwith, with the sensation of unreality one experiences in a nightmare, read the fulsome eulogy of the dead man. But the dead man was not here described as dead. The conventional phrases of the newspaper reporter, "Mr. Conway refused to be interviewed." "At his home it was said that Mr. Conway did not wish to add anything to the statement of his attorneys, who have completed the arrangements for the gift." All the evasions and artifices of men who have failed to see an important man were used.

Through the mist of incredulous amazement, Beckwith could gather only one impression. Conway had not been seen. No one had looked upon his living form to write of him recently. Beckwith knew why, of course. Conway was dead. But why, why had this gift been announced as from a living man?

With trembling fingers Beckwith spread out the remainder of the papers. Here and there he saw references to the gift. A monster sum was to be expended for fresh air outings for the children of the slums. Every reference spoke of the frequent benefactions of the man Beckwith knew was dead, but not one word or line referred to his murder.

True, there was no direct mention of a late interview with him, but on the other hand no faintest hint had escaped the editorial writers of the fact that he had been killed, and that his murderer had gone openly to a country from which he could not be extradited, where he was living in ease and comfort, defying the law to punish him.

When the last of the papers had been gone through, Beckwith

was in a frenzy. He had killed Conway, and the papers would not mention it! He felt almost as if he were being cheated, as, in a way, he was. A large part of his triumph was the public knowledge of his superiority to both Conway and Wells. To be deprived of that was infuriating, daunting.

Beckwith suddenly got up and went from the house, to walk heedlessly in the pouring rain and try to think what could have happened to set his plans awry. Such few brown-skinned folk as saw him shrugged their shoulders and murmured softly to one another. *Los Yanquis* were mad, though el Señor Beckwith had seemed less mad than they until now. But behold him walking in the downpour!

When he finally stumbled into his own house again, Beckwith was exhausted both mentally and physically. He made his way, dripping, into the room where he had left his newspapers. His wife rose and fled from the room when he appeared, leaving behind her the picture section at which she had been looking.

She read no English, and but little Spanish, but the brown-tinted pictures gave her childish pleasure. Beckwith paid no attention to her hasty flight, but slumped down in his chair and stared gloomily at the floor. Then, suddenly, a picture on the illustrated sheet grew clear and distinct. It was a picture of Hugh Conway, at the top of his stroke, about to strike a golf-ball. The legend beneath the picture read: "Hugh Conway, well-known multimillionaire, taking a vacation from business cares at Newport. He is shown driving off from the first tee in front of the clubhouse.

Beckwith, staring at the picture of the man whose life he had choked out a month before, caught his breath and began to swear at the printed sheet, hysterically, as he might have sworn at a ghost.

When the fruit steamer stopped on its northern trip, Beckwith took possession of a cabin. He did not quite understand why he was going to New York, but he was feverishly impatient for the ship to leave Bahia del Toro. He had a letter of credit in his pocket, and was determined to find out once and for all what had happened. If Conway had escaped him before, he would not escape again.

In his stateroom Beckwith carried the last batch of papers he had received, and spent much time reading and rereading the items concerning Conway. He weighed again and again each phrase in the accounts of Conway's munificent gift to charity, hoping to find therein some hint of Conway's death. He knew Conway was dead. He had choked Conway's life from him with his two hands. But why, why, why did not the papers announce the murder?

The ship steamed up the coast with incredible slowness. It put into Havana with nerve-racking deliberation. There were fresh papers to be secured there, but none of them told of the murder. Beckwith read them minutely, and as the steamer neared New York he came out on deck and paced back and forth, smoking incessantly, torturing his brain for an explanation of the silence of the newspapers.

His nerves were in shreds when they finally reached New York. He watched the forts swing by to his left, and the tall buildings of lower Manhattan rise from the water. The fixed expressionlessness of the Statue of Liberty irritated him. He was all impatience to be ashore and free to make his final investigations. What had happened that had prevented the press from learning of Conway's death? And why had they printed no word of his murder? The leisurely manner of the customs inspectors drove him nearly frantic. When he was at last free to go ashore he was trembling from sheer nervous tension.

He went down the gangplank, an olive-skinned steward carrying his bags. He pushed roughly through the crowd of people come to meet the voyagers, and closed his ears to the soft Spanish greetings. He failed altogether to see a motion-picture photographer cranking busily. He pressed free of the assembly of people, and turned impatiently to the steward behind him.

"Trouble you to come with me, sir," said a quiet voice at his elbow.

Two unimpressive figures in civilian clothes stood, one on either side. The hand of each was in his coat pocket, where a suggestive bulge warned against resistance.

"What the devil!" began Beckwith furiously, and stopped.

Wells was standing there, smiling sarcastically at him — Wells the commissioner of police.

"You're under arrest for Hugh Conway's murder, Beckwith," he said caustically.

A dozen or more delighted men watched the scene, cameras and notebooks busy. Beckwith saw the unmistakable signs of the reportorial trade. There was even a woman or two among them, "sob-sisters" beyond a doubt.

"We might as well make it a nice, dramatic moment, Beckwith," Wells said dryly. "I got your letter, pinned to Conway's breast. Kind of you to tell me where you were going, and that you couldn't be extradited. I wouldn't have got you but for that. I knew you'd look in the papers for news of your feat; as a matter of fact, you mentioned it in your letter, so I took the boys here into my confidence" — he nodded at the group of newspapermen — "and they agreed to help out. Their owners O.K.'d the scheme, and the murder was kept absolutely secret from the public and the press.

"We gave you two weeks to get worried, and then announced Conway's bequest to charities — it was really in his will — and printed a picture or so of him. You rose to the bait, all right. We couldn't touch you in Nueva Bolivia, but as soon as you boarded the steamer, we had you. We let you come on to New York alone, though, to save trouble. We're much obliged to you, I'm sure."

Beckwith suddenly understood. He had not won his revenge and freedom after all. He had not proven himself cleverer than Wells. He had lost, utterly and irreparably. He had been lured into the power of the law by nothing more than silence. But the thing that cut deepest into his heart, that made the cup of his humiliation run over, was a final remark of Wells. The reporters were listening intently.

"I guess that's all, boys," said Wells indulgently, "No more to be said. You'll have a good story for the evening editions. Beckwith couldn't resist playing to the gallery gods."

THE STREET OF
MAGNIFICENT DREAMS

There is a certain street in Burkton which might be called a street of magnificent dreams. There is in every town just such a street, or perhaps it is a park, and in the city of New York it is a curious mixture of bus stops and sidewalks that takes the place of a vantage point. But in Burkton it is a street — a quiet, elm-shaded thoroughfare with a white roadway in the middle, and plank sidewalks, and modest, comfortable homes on either side.

To look at it in the daytime, it seems quite an ordinary place, merely a succession of more or less well-kept lawns, with picket fences and occasional hedges, small houses, and — after school hours — playing children. But at night it is a pathway of dreams. At night the trees cast a deep, dim shadow. They meet above the roadway and darken it completely, and they shadow the walks to a dense and gentle gloom. From the flowerbeds and the lawns comes the scent of growing things.

From the darkness of the porches may come the red glow of an after-dinner cigar, or a girl's laugh, or perhaps a flood of inconsequential melody may tinkle out into the night. Fireflies flash their blue flames among the trees, possibly pursued by small and grubby hands, to be captured and imprisoned in glass bottles for some of the unknown purposes of childhood.

But on the walks — there are dreams and visions. Slender young girls in summery, white dresses walk shyly there with their sweethearts. Some of them talk gaily. Now and then those upon the porches will hear a little ripple of utterly carefree laughter. Some of them talk softly. Some of them pass slowly through the gloom with shining faces and gently intertwined fingers. And sometimes the young men will be speaking eagerly, confidently. They will be describing the visions they see.

The young girls, too, are seeing visions, but they do not speak of them. They look with soft eyes into the future and see the happiness that will infallibly come to them, and they see homes, perhaps, which are not quite as imposing as the visions of the young men beside them, but are vastly more desirable. And then, too, they may see other things, which are just a little more vague but infinitely to be hoped for. Very small things, pink and white, and miraculously alive.

These are the visions that are seen upon the street of magnificent dreams in Burkton.

Alicia Blake had walked upon that street, years before, and

now she lived upon its edge, but the dreams were gone. Dreams have a way of fading. She sat upon her porch, feeling the cool of the summer night. Before her gate passed two of the dreamers — carefree dreamers, these. The girl was laughing at some jest of her escort. Alicia listened with a troubled brow. She could see what would come to those two who walked in the gloom, and it might be good fortune or it might be bad, but inevitably it would not possess the beauty of those radiant phantasms of lovers' dreaming. There was always disillusionment. She knew.

Her husband was sitting but a little way from her, his feet propped luxuriously upon the railing of the porch, smoking his after-dinner cigar and gazing at the strollers with an untroubled brow.

"I like to watch them, Alicia," he said presently, as a dim white figure passed slowly before the gate. "It's rather — it reminds me of old times. We used to walk like that."

"Yes," said Alicia slowly, "we did."

She lay back in her chair, curiously unhappy. No one had ever known such dreams as they had had. Harry was to become an important man in Burkton. The road was clear before him to the presidency of his firm. In five years, they had devoutly believed, they would be well-to-do. In ten years they would be wealthy. And in fifteen years, they foresaw infallibly, they would be spending their summers abroad. Harry would be one of the big men of the town. There was nothing to hold him back. He was ambitious, he was capable, and — he would have Alicia to help him. It had seemed very certain, in those days.

A young man's voice came from the obscurity beneath the trees.

"And in five years —" he was saying earnestly, confidently.

His tone dropped to a murmur. There was a little speck of grayish white beside him — a girl, of course.

Alicia closed her eyes. The fragrance of her husband's cigar came faintly to her nostrils. That, after all, was the measure of their success. Now he could smoke cigars. When they were first married he had smoked a pipe and doled out his tobacco sparingly. Now they owned their home. They would never have to fear poverty. But for the rest —

Harry grunted suddenly.

"Forgot to tell you, 'Lecia," he said idly. "I heard from Tom Kerry today. He's been taken into partnership."

Alicia did not answer. Harry expected none. Her unhappiness increased just a little. Harry had had the chance that Tom Kerry had taken. The opening for which he had commended the other man had been offered first to him. If he had taken it —

Instead, he was sitting upon his front porch, smoking quietly, quite untroubled, while the business for which he had been working for ten years was changing hands. It was being bought in by a larger concern, a million-dollar house, and Harry might be kept on, or he might be dropped.

She asked a sudden question. "What about the office, Harry?"

He shifted his position easily. "The papers were to be signed tonight, I understand. The deal's gone through. By tomorrow I'll have a new set of bosses."

He smiled to himself in the darkness.

Alicia felt a curious uneasiness. "How about changes, Harry?"

His tone was casual.

"There'll be a few, I suppose. We've got some good men."

Alicia clenched her hands, unseen. That was Harry's way. He did not push himself. Three or four times he had been consulted on details of management. More often than that he had been consulted on promotions. He had commended other men — even younger men — for advancement over his own head. True, they had invariably made good, but Harry could have done the same. He had became a plugger, a steady, dependable man, instead of a brilliant one. And there was no reason for it.

"No danger of my being out of a place long," he added suddenly, smiling. "No need to worry."

"I know."

But the unhappiness persisted. It was quite true that he need not fear unemployment. He had helped too many men now in positions of power. Tom Kerry was but one of many whom Harry had given a boost, and Tom Kerry was now making easily twice what Harry earned.

The procession on the street of magnificent dreams continued. Always the dreamers walked in pairs. They walked beneath the overhanging trees, and some of them talked gaily, and some talked softly, and some passed slowly along the way with shining faces and gently intertwined fingers. All of them saw visions of the future, a radiant future, most marvelously certain to be achieved.

There was a little pause, and a young man and girl walked alone.

The young man's voice came, strained a little, bitterly unhappy. "But — but what can we do?" he asked despairingly. "What can we do?"

The girl was silent, but her head was bent.

They passed on in silence. Only the faint murmur of the young man's voice came back despairingly.

"That's Jack Grahame," said Harry suddenly, "and I suppose that's little Milly with him."

Alicia nodded.

"She lives with her aunt, you know, and her parents are dead. Her aunt makes her do all the housework. She doesn't have a very pleasant time."

Harry puffed at his cigar for an instant, "I rather imagine they feel pretty badly," he said reflectively. "Jack has a rather poor job. He couldn't possibly marry on his salary. And Milly isn't in very happy surroundings. If they're in love with each other it must be pretty hard on them."

Alicia meditated an instant. "No, they can't marry now, but it would be splendid for them if they could."

She felt a certain vague sympathy for the pair, but soon dropped back into her own depressed musing. She and Harry had walked along this street of dreams, and had dreamed of the future. Harry was to be a big man in Burkton. He was to be a success. It had looked so perfectly certain. He was young and ambitious, and had Alicia to help him.

But he had helped other men instead. There were a dozen of them, in different lines, that he had helped to get their start. He had got Tom Kerry the position that had led up to his present partnership in the firm he worked for. He had loaned another young man the money to start in business — and the business was now a big one. A third he had urged for promotion over his own head, and that man was a vice-president of the Amalgamated Wood Products Company, the firm that was buying out his own company now.

There were others — many others. They had been clerks under him, and he had trained them and shown them the path.

And they had all outstripped him.

There was no reason for it. Harry was as good as any of the men he had assisted, though they were successes and he was a failure. Alicia winced a little at the branding word. There was no escaping it, though. Harry was a failure. The others had gone ahead, and he had stayed behind. They could afford European trips, if they chose, but Harry could not. In justice, Alicia did not wish for foreign travel as a thing in itself. She wished for it as a symbol of success, as a fruition of those radiant visions they had seen when they walked together in the dusk.

Harry was puffing thoughtfully upon his cigar.

"Tom Kerry said," he remarked suddenly, "that he'd heard our firm was being bought out. He told me they could use me in his line, if I cared to come. Said they had a vacancy."

Alicia felt another little pang. Tom Kerry had been a clerk under Harry, and was now offering to become his employer. It was a symbol of Harry's failure. And it would be a good position, too. Tom Kerry would be grateful. The thing that rankled was the reversal of places. Harry had once been above Tom Kerry. Now their relative importance was neatly inverted. Harry had been outstripped, and the fault was all his own. He had failed of self-assertion. He had failed of ambition. Despite Alicia, he had failed.

II.

Those who walked along the way saw visions. Heart-breakingly sure of the future, they faced it eagerly. A young man and a young girl. A young girl and a young man. Always neatly paired, always eagerly confident, they strolled together in the dusk and talked gaily, or softly, or walked in silence with fingers inter-twined.

All but two of these strollers. Jack Grahame and little Milly returned, slowly, unhappily.

Milly was crying quietly, trying not to make any noise.

"They make Milly do all the housework, eh?" said Harry suddenly. "I know that aunt of hers."

They saw a little movement, as if Jack had clumsily tried to comfort the girl by his side.

"Loving each other," went on Harry whimsically, "and unhappy, and not able to marry. Jack!" He raised his voice a little. "Jack! Come here a moment."

The two figures halted. There was a moment's murmured conference, and then Jack came up the path alone.

"What is it, Mr. Blake?"

They could not see his face from the porch, but his tone was weary and forlorn and full of a youthful despair.

"Wanted to talk to you a minute, Jack," said Harry. "Isn't that Milly by the gate?" He added the question with a diplomatic air of casualness.

"Y-yes." The young man hesitated. "She's not feeling very cheerful," he explained with something of defiance. "She doesn't want to talk, just now."

"Bring her up here, Jack," said Harry gently. "I want to speak to her, too."

The young man stood irresolute for a moment, then went down to the gate, and presently returned with Milly reluctantly in his wake.

"You know the plant's being sold tonight, Jack," announced Harry.

He nodded gloomily. "That means new bosses," he said desperately, "and no chance for a raise for me."

Harry smiled a little in the obscurity.

"It isn't the best thing," he observed, "to think of your work in terms of wages, but let it pass. Jack, aren't you engaged to Milly?"

"Y-yes, I am," said Jack defiantly.

Harry nodded.

"You can't marry on your present pay, Jack, and you really aren't worth more where you are. It isn't your line. Jack, how'd you like a new job?"

Jack stared at him.

"I'm going to be fired?" he asked unsteadily.

Harry shook his head.

"I got a letter today from a man I know," he went on. "He has a vacancy in his business. I can get you the place, if you like. It won't pay you as much as it would me, but if you make good —"

Jack drew a deep, quick breath.

"Would it — could I —" He stopped.

Harry stood up.

"Come in the house, Jack. I'll show you the letter."

They went indoors. There was silence for a long minute. Milly stood there in the dusk, her head bent a little, struggling to keep back the tears. She had not really heard what had been said. A sudden wave of sympathy swept over Alicia.

"Come here, Milly," she said quietly. "And if you want to cry — I won't listen."

III.

Out on the street of magnificent dreams the couples went by, dim shadows in the gloom, while in the darkness of the porch little Milly wept in a sudden passion of despair. She had been walking upon the street of visions, and had not been able to see the marvelous panoramas that the street contained for others. She and Jack had been walking there, and could not imagine rose-tinted castles, nor iridescent dreams. They could see only the shadows, and it had disheartened them.

And then Jack came out quickly, and took Milly incontinently in his arms. His face was glowing. He was almost incoherent with happiness. Harry came more slowly after, and watched with a whimsical smile as Jack babbled out his marvelous tidings.

"Why — why, it means everything, Milly!" he said breathlessly. "I'll tell you all about it. Mr. Blake —" He was anxious to be alone with Milly, so he could point out to her the marvelous thing that was before them. He hesitated upon the step of the porch.

"I — I — you understand, Mr. Blake?" He fumbled for words, and crushed Harry's hand. "I feel as if I'd like to say — God bless you, sir."

He finished shamefacedly, and went down the path with Milly. His voice was hurried now, in explanation. It was exultant. And as they passed slowly along the street of dreams it came back to them, eager and confident. "Milly — in five years —"

Harry nodded, smiling, as they passed from view.

"And he'll make good," he commented. "He'll fit in where Tom Kerry'll put him."

Alicia was silent. A sudden unworthy thought occurred to her, Harry might need the position he had just given to Jack. His firm was being sold. With the new management he might lose his position. They need have no fear, but still —

Harry reached out his hand and found Alicia's.

"How about it, 'Lecia?"

"I'm — glad you did it," she said uncertainly. "But, Harry, when the new management comes in —"

He smiled obscurely to himself.

"We'll worry about that when it happens," he told her.

Unhappy, she let him hold her hand. She could never feel that she did not love him. It was only that she felt that he had failed. He had showed so many others the way to success. He had made so many successes for others, but none for himself.

A white, brilliant light swept suddenly down the tree-lined avenue, silvering the lower branches and etching vividly the tree trunks. A couple just before their door was outlined sharply. For an instant Alicia saw the line of a girl's throat and chin. The girl was laughing. And then as the motorcar moved she was dropped back into darkness again.

Curiously speckled, the edges of the headlight glow moved and wavered as the car drew nearer. It slowed, as if the chauffeur were looking for an individual house. It stopped, and there was the faint murmur of voices, above the soft purring of a throttled-down motor. And then it came on, slowed again, and stopped before their door. The light within the limousine was snapped off. A door clicked and then slammed, and their front gate squeaked a little as a figure came into their yard. He came up toward the house, a small, wispy man whose features were hard to make out in the darkness.

"Mr. Blake?"

Harry rose and extended his hand.

Alicia was bewildered.

"Told you I'd probably want to see you tonight," said the strange voice. "How do you do?"

Harry turned to Alicia.

"'Lecia, I want you to know Mr. Grover. He's the president of the Amalgamated. My wife."

The wispy man acknowledged the introduction. Harry motioned him to a chair.

"Would you rather talk indoors?"

"It's better out here." Harry's new employer sat down and stared out at the soft dimness. He sniffed at the scents of growing things, and at Alicia's flowers near the porch. "I wish I had a place like this. By James, I do! I begin to understand you now."

Alicia was growing more and more confused. The man was a millionaire, several times over, and envying Harry his house.

"You know why I came, Blake," he said abruptly. "I hinted at it today. Didn't know when we'd finish with those silly papers, so I thought I'd drop by. Going early tomorrow morning. We've closed the deal. The Amalgamated takes over your firm, lock, stock and barrel."

Alicia felt utterly bewildered. Harry was no more than a department head in his firm. Why was the new owner —

"Now you know, Blake," went on Grover quietly, "why we bought you people out. Your plant hasn't been dangerous to us, but it was getting along a little too well. And we found out why. It has probably the best set of executives in the country. We wanted those men — but more than that, we wanted the system that made 'em. And you know what that system was."

"I'm afraid I don't," admitted Harry, smiling,

"By James!" exclaimed the visitor indignantly. "If you don't, I don't know who does! Look here! One of the vice-presidents of the Amalgamated says you're the greatest man in the United States for picking out and developing good timber for high-priced men. It probably isn't modest of him to say so, because you picked him out. Remember?"

"Pretty good man," admitted Harry.

"We've got one or two more who worked under you. They're good men. We're paying the least of them five thousand a year. We're short of five thousand a year men and we're shorter of ten thousand a year men, and we're in howling, crying need of some twenty thousand a year men. There aren't enough men who're really good! And we need 'em!"

He settled back in his chair and waved his hand.

"Now, you can pick them, and you can develop them. That's why I want you. There are a dozen ten to twenty thousand a year men who swear that you set them on their feet. If you can do it for them, you can do it for some others, and I can use half a dozen men right now if they're good enough for salaries like that. If they can earn it I'll pay it to 'em, but I can't find 'em!"

"We've got some pretty good men —" began Harry,

"Piffle," muttered the millionaire inelegantly. "I know what I'm talking about. That's why you're going to manage this plant for me."

Alicia drew in her breath sharply. Harry to manage the plant!

"I'm going to run this place as a college," continued Grover. "This plant I've bought tonight is going to be a supply station for men for big jobs. If I hit on a likely man I'm going to send him to you to be polished up — though he won't know it. You've made a dozen successful men. I need successful men.

"You're going to run this place and develop every bit of worth-while timber you see. And as fast as you develop 'em I'm going to take 'em away from you. You know what a man's good for — how, I don't know. You picked out most of the men who're above you now. They're good, but you're better. So — I expect to find vice-presidents and executives coming out of this plant. And in the meantime your salary will be multiplied by four and you're in charge of the place. That suit you?"

Harry debated.

"I don't know that I can do anything special," he answered tentatively. "Only, now and then, when I find a good subordinate —"

Grover chuckled and stood up.

"That's just the trick," he said enthusiastically. "When you find a good subordinate — have you any bad ones now?"

"No-o," admitted Harry. "They're all pretty good."

"Which may be an accident," retorted Grover, holding out his hand, "but may not. It's just possible that you make 'em good. I'm banking on that anyway. You take charge of the plant Monday week."

Harry went dawn to the car with him. Alicia was almost afraid to believe what she had heard. Harry — her Harry — to be in absolute charge. He'd be one of the big men of Burkton. He'd be — he'd be —

He came up the pathway whistling.

"Had a hint of that yesterday, 'Lecia," he said apologetically, "but I didn't want to mention it. It might not have worked out."

Alicia was breathless.

"But, Harry!" she exclaimed. "It's wonderful! Why — why —"

"I've been sort of a failure up to now," said Harry reflectively. "I haven't made much of a success. But in five years —"

A sudden light burst on Alicia. Down before her front gate couples were walking upon the street of magnificent dreams. They saw the future laid out before them, marvelously beautiful and radiant, and most infallibly certain to come about as they desired. And Alicia smiled.

"You a failure, Harry?" she repeated. She put her hands in his. "If you haven't made a success of yourself, it's been because you were making successes of other men. And you've surely made a success of that!"

But Harry still rubbed his chin reflectively. "In five years —" he began. "I say, 'Lecia, let's take a little walk up and down the street."

And then they, too, slipped out beneath the trees. And Harry's voice became eager and confident. They were walking for the second time upon the street of magnificent dreams, and Harry was describing the visions he saw there. They were radiant and beautiful visions, and Alicia listened with soft eyes. She felt very proud, for she was marvelously sure that *these* dreams were infallibly certain to be fulfilled.

NERVE

The fairgrounds receded swiftly, and then more slowly. The earth below flattened out abruptly, while the horizon seemed to rise until Berry Barnes was floating in the center of a vast bowl of verdant earth, with the blue sky arching above. He sat at ease on the slender bar of the trapeze and looked down, smiling.

He had a passion for the heights. To look down, down, down at the earth held a sort of fascination for him — a fascination that was wholly different from the suicidal vertigo so many people experience. Over his head a huge cotton bag billowed in ungainly bulk. It stank of the gasoline fumes of the fire that had inflated it. From where Berry sat he could look up through its narrow neck into a cavernous, smoky interior.

He loved the whole thing, the whole game of his daring ascents and parachute jumps, from the first laying out of the sooty bag on the green grass — with the center buoyed up between two poles at the sides — through every phase of the inflation and flight of the dirty-gray balloon. He loved the furnace that inflated his pet. He loved his last, always dramatic leap for the trapeze bar as the great bag was released and shot upward into the air. He loved the peace of the heights, the stillness broken only by the increasingly faint blaring of the band that always played "Up in a Balloon, Boys," as he rose, dangling on that slender, ineffective looking trapeze bar.

But most of all, he loved to look down from the heights at the earth below, swinging back and forth as he watched for a favorable landing-place. When he had selected his spot, there was the slender rope, the knife-cord, by his side. A pull, the cord was cut, and then — a breathless rush downward, fifty, a hundred, sometimes two hundred feet, before the parachute opened and his fall was stayed with a slight jar. After that he floated down beneath the suddenly blossomed flower above him. It was life, the quintessence of life. The thrill of danger, the intoxication of the heights, and that rapturous dash earthward at the end — those were the most perfect moments of Berry's life.

Only Anne knew how he loved it all, but only Anne knew how her heart constricted when he shot downward from the cooling balloon. Perhaps the parachute would not open. Perhaps some rope would give way. Perhaps — perhaps — She lived in an agony of fear for him.

He laughed at her. He had made two hundred ascents before she married him, and nearly as many since, but she never saw him rise into the air without a terrible fear taking possession of her. Her greatest dread was that the parachute would not open. Some day that quick downward rush would not be checked. The little black dot that meant her husband would fall with the trailing bud of canvas behind it, and the bud would not blossom out. Swiftly and more swiftly he would fall, and the parachute would not open. She awoke sometimes in the middle of the night, crying out in terror. Berry could hardly comfort her.

He never told her of his own chief anxiety. Down beside him there ran a slender rope, connecting above with a sharp knife. When he pulled the rope the knife severed the cord that held his parachute and himself to the smoking, stinking bag. If ever that knife failed him, and the parachute was not released —

It was the one appalling thought in his mind. The bag above him would slowly cool, then more quickly. It would shrivel a little, and begin to droop toward the earth. He would sink, at first slowly, then swiftly. The bag above him would cease to be a bulging, ungainly object. It would become a slim, writhing, snake-like thing. He would drop.

Once he had seen that happen to another balloonist. The man had jumped clear two hundred feet up. When they came to him he was not a pleasant sight to look upon. Berry resolutely thrust that thought from his mind, only examining the knife in person before each ascent.

The big tents of the fair had grown small and toy-like. The blaring of the band was indistinct. The only noises he could hear were faint cheerings and the more penetrating sound of auto horns. He estimated his height with a practiced eye. Twelve hundred feet; fifteen hundred feet; eighteen hundred feet. He began to look down for his landing-space.

A big, clear field caught his eye. In a moment or two he would be over it. He waited, swinging back and forth on the trapeze bar and watching the earth flow slowly by beneath him. He smiled unconsciously. No one could tell what this meant to him. Even Anne only guessed. If she knew how he loved these moments up aloft she would never again beg him to take up some less dangerous trade.

The field he had selected was below him. He watched a moment, allowing for his drift during the parachute drop. His hand was on the rope that would cut him free from the balloon. He looked to the left. The sand-bag that would overturn the bag when he had deserted it swung free. He glanced up. The parachute was in its proper position, not tangled, in every way as experience dictated. He pulled the knife-cord. Nothing happened.

He still swung below the bag. A quick cold sweat broke out on his face. He pulled again and again. The rope did not part. His heart seemed to stop beating. Eighteen hundred feet up, under a cooling balloon, and unable to free himself. He craned his neck upward, but could not see the knife that should have released him.

In a flash he visualized the bag shrinking, then finally collapsing, then the dash downward, the parachute opening fitfully, only to be crushed and tangled in the flapping bag, and finally Anne being brought to where he would be lying crushed on the ground. The pictures snapped before his eyes like the scenes of a movie. He groaned and shut his eyes. Then, quite suddenly, a vision came before him.

It was that morning. Anne and he were sitting at breakfast in the rather dingy hotel that was the best the county seat afforded. The waitress served them with a little awe in her manner. He was that reckless daredevil who made the parachute jumps at the fair, and she always felt that perhaps this would be the last meal he would eat on earth. The other people in the dining room looked at him curiously. They all knew who he was and wondered at his daring. They did not know how he loved every bit of the game. They wondered what queer trait made him so reckless.

Anne was pale. She had waked in the middle of the night, crying out in fear for him.

"What's the matter, Anne?" Berry asked. "You look as if you didn't feel well."

"I don't," she said reluctantly. She looked at him, and her eyes filled with tears, though she tried to smile bravely.

"Frightened again?" he asked.

She nodded.

"I never stop being frightened," she said in an oddly quiet voice.

"Oh, piffle, Anne!" he exclaimed. "There isn't anything to be worried about. I'm careful. You know I'm careful."

She shook her head wordlessly. She tried not to bother him about her fears, but she did wish she had not this constant prospect before her, of his horrible death at any time.

"Carefulness isn't much of a comfort, Berry."

"Now listen, dear," he said coaxingly. "I've made nearly four hundred ascents without a serious accident. One time I sprained my ankle in landing. Once I went up when the wind was high and was dragged along the ground a bit by the parachute when I struck. A broken rib that time. Look at that record, Anne. Think of the people who are killed in every big city by automobiles and streetcars. I'm almost afraid to go into a big town!"

He stopped, hoping she would smile. Instead, she only looked at her plate and halfheartedly tried to eat.

"Lord, Anne," he went on cheerfully, "when I think of the perils to which people in cities are exposed — I'm positively a danger dodger! And anyway," he added pleadingly, "you know how I dote on the game. You know how I love the whole business, from the stink of the furnace that inflates the old bag, to the last least littlest thrill of the jump. You wouldn't have me lose that, would you?"

"You know how I love you," said Anne softly. "Do you think I like to be afraid I'm going to lose you?"

"But you aren't," protested Berry with a laugh. "I'm safe as can be, Anne. I never take any unnecessary risks."

"I know," said Anne. "But, oh, Berry, if there weren't any 'necessary' ones!"

The vision vanished, and Berry was again sitting high in the air beneath his old gray balloon, that had carried him aloft so many times, and now seemed to be holding him up for a last few moments before dropping him to his death. The vision of himself and Anne at breakfast had been instantaneous, merely a flash of memory that carried him back to the talk at the table. He jerked agonizedly at the knife-cord. The rope that held him fast remained unparted. The balloon was rising sluggishly now. The air within was still hot enough to carry him a little higher, but was cooling steadily.

Berry ground his teeth together. He was not afraid. He had faced death too often to feel a touch of cowardice now that it had come so close. It was only that a glimpse of what his death would mean to Anne had suddenly swept over him. He had married her a year before.

She was clerking in a store in New York, one of the shops that show such startling values for their prices. It was known among thrifty shoppers as the cheapest store at which to buy. Anne knew why. The advertisements said it gave great values because of the reduction of overhead expenses and the consequent decrease in the cost of goods to the purchaser. Anne knew that "overhead expenses" included, among other things, the salaries it paid to its clerks.

They were young girls mostly, and they hated the store with a consuming hatred. To cut down the cost of operation it paid them salaries on which they could barely keep body and soul together — this was in the days before the war, remember — and sometimes it did become a question of keeping body or soul alive. Berry had married Anne from behind a counter.

Sensing the growing sluggishness of the balloon above him, Berry remembered with a groan the story she had told him after their marriage, of the terrible, monotonous struggle with poverty, with the ever-present problem of getting enough to eat and still maintaining the standard of neatness the store required. She had no relatives to help her out. She had to fend for herself. She could not be a stenographer or a typist — she had no training. And the store was a deadly grind, a monotonous torture.

With Berry dead, Anne would have no one to care for her. They had saved a little money, a very little. Berry earned it so easily it hardly seemed worthwhile to save. Anne might live on their savings for a year — perhaps. Then the store again, no friends, no family, and a grinding poverty, lasting until she gave up.

Berry seemed to see her coming out of some employees' entrance, buffeted by the other clerks, tired out, her clothes shabby.

A great rage swept over him, rage at himself. He had been so absorbed in the joys of his work that he had neglected to provide for her. He had thought of the fun he was having, glorying in the thrill of his flight and the breathless dash downward in the parachute, thinking only of himself while she had been fearing for him constantly. Berry still was not afraid for himself. He was as good as dead, and he knew it. He ignored that, thinking only of Anne.

He glanced up at the balloon. It was cooling noticeably. Long wrinkles began to appear in the lower part of the bag. Berry jerked automatically at the knife-cord, his face deathly pale and his forehead beaded with sweat. Anne. Only Anne. His own death was nothing, but Anne would care. He remembered how she had looked when he was in the hospital with those broken ribs of his.

The utter pallor of her face while the doctor poked investigating fingers about his chest had distracted Berry's attention even from his pain. The agony of apprehension that was reflected in her expression had fascinated him. Berry had felt a little awe when the doctor pronounced the triviality of his injuries. Her face had been radiant beyond any radiance he had seen before.

The balloon was cooling. Somehow, Berry sensed the loss of buoyancy even before it began to droop sluggishly toward the earth. It would not be more than a minute or so more now. The long wrinkles in the lower part were more prominent. Berry's arm automatically jerked and jerked at the knife-cord. The balloon sank slowly, and then more quickly. Berry was not afraid for himself, but only for Anne; for what his death would mean to her. He had been selfish, utterly so. For his own part, the joy he had had in his ballooning was payment even for the death he was now to meet, but Anne —

The balloon had ceased to be globular and was sinking rapidly. Berry looked up for the last time. It was a wrinkled, emaciated object. It began to flap back and forth, heavily and awkwardly. Berry groaned and closed his eyes. One arm held fast to the side rope of the trapeze. The other jerked unconsciously at the knife-cord. Down, down, the bag flapping more loudly and violently. Suddenly he began to fall with a rush. This was the end. Anne —

He gasped. His drop had been checked with a soft jar. He looked up, unbelieving. The parachute was open, blossomed out above his head. He no longer saw the flapping balloon. Incredulously he saw that every bit of the open parachute was bathed in sunlight. He was free of the huge bag that had threatened him! The knife, failing to cut, had at last chafed its way through the holding-rope.

For an instant Berry was faint with the revulsion, then he recovered and looked down. An open field, small, but amply large for his needs, lay directly below him. He made his landing skilfully.

Forman, his helper who inflated the balloon, greeted him with a grin and an outstretched hand.

"Gee, boss," he said thankfully, "I thought you was a goner then. When the old bag begun to flap I says to myself I'd seen you go up for the last time."

"You have," said Berry briefly.

"What's that?" demanded Forman incredulously. "You ain't goin' up no more?"

"I'm cured," said Berry with a smile. "No more."

A puzzled look came over Forman's face.

"Lost your nerve?" he asked.

Berry shook his head. Forman could not be made to understand. He would never be able to grasp that Berry had already devised a new type of parachute-release that simply could not fail — and never intended to use it. He would never understand that Berry, in spite of his recent extraordinarily narrow escape, still felt that in giving up his ascents to make sure that Anne would always be cared for and happy he was giving up the thing he cared most for in all the world.

"No, I haven't lost my nerve," he said with a half smile at Forman. "I —" He shrugged his shoulders slightly. "Where's my wife?"

STORIES OF THE HUNGRY COUNTRY

The Case of the Dona Clotilde

If you look at Ticao from the sea, you will say it is beautiful. It is beautiful partly because it is old. The Cathedral of Our Lady of Mercy was built by black slaves — sweating in chains, and with their overseers' whips perpetually flicking their backs — nearly three hundred years ago. The great fortress that is great no longer, and is now used only to confine political prisoners from Portugal, was built when the discovery of America was still an interesting topic. Even the Governor's palace is very, very old. Many of the governors prefer more modern residences and build them for themselves, but sometimes an official will be found brave enough to endure the dampness of the thick walls for the sake of their coolness, and the crawling things in the cracks and crannies for the sake of the real opulence and dignity of the building.

All those three buildings — and the empty-windowed hospital that was a gift from a Queen of Portugal — help to make the city beautiful, but they alone do not create the beauty. No; Ticao is very old, and most of it was built before the days of galvanized iron, so the roofs are of tiles, and are beautiful. Then, Ticao has that other quality that is found only in very old places — atmosphere. Instinctively, wandering through the crooked streets of the old city, you know that here is a place of age and assurance, the ways of which will be hard to change.

Once a city acquires that quality of atmosphere, wise men who visit it inquire into its traditions and adopt them temporarily. One may defy codes of morals, or codes of ethics, but punishment for violation of traditions is sure. Ticao was once very wicked. Now everything that is done there has the sanction of the law, but its traditions remain unchanged. In Ticao you must do as the Ticaoans, or the city and all the generations at its back will contrive that you suffer for your temerity. Position and place will avail you nothing. Be you the meanest *servaçal*, or even the Governor, you must live up to the traditions of Ticao. The city is assured in its ways, but sometimes it is kind to the newcomer who would change them, pointing out gently but unmistakably that the old ways are best and must continue.

There was the Dona Clotilde. She was the Governor's wife, and sought to change the ways of old Ticao. To her, the city was kind. She was most gently dissuaded from her project. There is a rule in the regulations of the *Minesterio das Colónias* that soldiers and officials must not take their wives to Ticao because they die there and it is annoying; but from this provision the Governor is exempt. His wife is legally entitled to all the fevers and plagues of the coast, should she decide to accompany her husband to his colony, and the Dona Clotilde elected to do just that. The Governor's predecessor had been killed by my acquaintance José in a manner I have related, and as a result the Governor took up his residence in the official Governor's palace. To that abode he brought, his bride when, after three years in office, he married a noble lady of Portugal.

I do not know what the Dona Clotilde expected of Ticao. Perhaps she expected to find there the more or less gay life of a provincial capital, of the society of which she would be the head by virtue of her position as the Governor's wife. Perhaps the Governor actually told her what Ticao was like, but I do not think he expatiated upon the fact that the only white women in the city were the sallow wives of traders and sometimes the wife of a missionary come down from the interior. He assuredly did not explain to her that because of the prohibition mentioned before, none of the officials had brought their wives, but instead had established ménages after the time-honored custom of Ticao. The city knows that men were not made to live alone, and looks indulgently on masculine frailty and feminine slavery.

I should explain that last word, I think. There are no more slaves in Ticao, but there are many, many contract laborers. There are vast differences between the two names in the eyes of the law, but to the observer there is no difference at all. Undoubtedly a scholar of the law would discover that the money paid by the employer-owner of the male and female slaves to the Arab and Portuguese slave-drivers who bring the blacks to the coast is simply a generous reimbursement of the cost of such transport, and it is equally certain that a scholar of the law would note many differences between the legal status of the former *escravas* and the present *servaçaes*. But to the ignorant person who merely owns a number of such slaves, the difference is imperceptible.

Whatever the Governor told the Dona Clotilde before he brought her to Ticao, she learned something of the true state of affairs afterward. Her personal maid was a brown-skinned girl for whom the Governor had paid over a hundred dollars two years before — and women for agricultural service are worth hardly more than seventy to eighty in Ticao, though the prices are higher on the islands. When the Governor brought a white wife to Ticao, Lobara was reduced to the rank of a house servant. The Governor's cook was a gigantic black whose back still bore the marks of the *sjambok* used in "taming" him. The first time the Dona Clotilde left the Governor's palace after her arrival in Ticao she saw two native women reaping the benefits of Christianity and civilization by being driven through the streets with blows of a heavy cudgel in the hands of the slave major-domo of their owner.

In course of time Dona Clotilde became acquainted with very many of the customs that have grown up in and about the city of Ticao. She heard the slaves humming the song:

> *"He has passed Ondumba ya Maria,"*

with its ghastly refrain:

> *"Ohee, ohee, I fear him now no more,*
> *He's gone to San Felipe,"*

every time a gang of slaves was marched along the long sandpit to take the steamer for the islands. She gathered some faint idea of the consuming horror of the slavery on those islands. I am told that she bought a little slave girl from the wife of one of the traders in Ticao, and found the girl's back literally raw from blows of a whip. The trader's wife had been in the habit of venting her spite on the girl.

Lobara, too, opened the Dona Clotilde's eyes to many things. When one has been the Governor's favorite for nearly two years, it must be annoying at least to be superseded by a pale white woman, and still worse to be assigned to be her slave. Lobara had found some consolation in the attentions of the huge cook, on whom she had looked with favor for a long time but to whom she had not dared be kind; but that was not a sufficient recompense for the loss of position she had sustained. It is not unusual for a native woman, on finding favor in the eyes of her master, to assume insufferable airs to the rest of her kind. Sometimes they suffer keenly, but the native woman's position is not high among the natives themselves, and when they are not set to work in the fields they suffer vastly less from the change to slavery under the white than under native men.

The Dona Clotilde was a tall woman for a Portuguese, with thin nostrils and imperious mouth that spoke of energy. She was not very clever, however. Had there been in Ticao a society of the sort the average provincial capital boasts, she would have been quite satisfied. Her energy — such as it was — would have expended itself in social functions. But her associates were half a dozen jaded, weary traders' wives, inured to the coast and all the customs of the coast, exchanging venomous gossip, constantly split into cliques even among their small number, but never quarreling irrevocably because of that small number and the need for each other's society. The Dona Clotilde could not organize society among so few. It was impossible to establish exclusiveness, because there were so few to exclude. Feminine society seems to preen itself not on the people it contains, but on the people it snubs. The Dona Clotilde became bored.

The Governor should have sent her back to Portugal. There she would have had a certain amount of prestige from being the wife of a Colonial Governor; she could have moved grandly among the wives of similar officials, and could have gotten into the usual amount of respectable mischief from the mischief-making that married women do. Instead, she stayed on in Ticao, living in shabby, moldy grandeur in the huge, battered governmental palace, giving a tea or something of the sort once a week, and being thoroughly bored. She had her first few attacks of fever, comforted herself with the belief that she was being a martyr to her duty in remaining with her husband at his post, and gradually the idea grew in her mind that she should exert her influence upon her husband in his duties. That is an idea that is very strong among Anglo-Saxon women, but so far the Latin races have to a great extent escaped it.

The duties of the Governor are principally those of officially closing his eyes to all the extortion and cruelty of the various officials under his direction, urging on the gathering of slaves — which you must remember are technically know as "*servaçaes*," or contract laborers — and seeing to it that he secures his perquisites as they become due. Once upon a time he was a person of great importance, because Ticao was the center of the slave trade with Cuba and Brazil. Then his staff was very large and was kept very busy. Now he has but little to do, as the dying trade in local products has become a lifeless, commonplace thing, and the still thriving trade in slaves for the coast and the islands is very competently attended to by the slave traders, both individuals and regularly incorporated companies.

The Dona Clotilde could find little with which to meddle. In divers and obscure ways her husband collected sums from the slave agents and from the traders who sold the fiery sugar-cane rum to the free natives. He audited with great care the records which showed the number of *contratos* recorded — which means the records which listed the blacks legally made slaves to the whites — because there was a small fee which went to him for every such contract recorded. Beyond this he had little to do. If it be true that he governs best who governs least, then the governors of Ticao must be admirable men. The most popular Governor is he who governs not at all, but leaves the natives to the tender mercy of the Portuguese, who enslave them and set them to work in their *roças*. If the Governor who brought the Dona Clotilde to Ticao could be said to have a policy at all, it was simply that of upholding the traders when they debauched the natives with their poisonous rum, upholding the soldiers when they made them- selves a scourge to the natives, and upholding the slave traders when they enslaved the natives.

The Dona Clotilde should not have attempted to interfere with her husband. He was gradually becoming accustomed to respectable domesticity. Her interference merely increased the speed with which that accustomedness became disgust. When I first saw the Dona Clotilde, she had just arrived in Ticao. Like everyone else, I paid my respects in the most formal fashion and was received with a curious mingling of hauteur and perplexity. As the Governor's wife, she felt she should be a little stiff until she was sure which of the inhabitants should be received cordially. The paucity of white people made any real exclusiveness impos- sible.

I remember a dinner the Governor gave to which practically all the wholly white population came. We gathered in the moldy state dining room where formerly a brilliant court had dined. We were a motley company of people. The two consuls of which Ticao boasts came, and lent dignity to the occasion. Three or four mili- tary officers came, resplendent in slightly tarnished gold lace. The short, fat Governor sat lumpily at the head of the table beside his wife and drank heavily. The tarnished officers drank heavily. The half dozen or so of traders' wives came, sallow and worn by the climate, and either watched their husbands jealously or tried des- perately to inject a note of sophisticated gaiety into the gathering. The slaves brought in the courses and stood behind our chairs in a shabby attempt at splendor. The Dona Clotilde watched us in puzzled bewilderment This was far from the official society she must have expected.

I went to the islands soon after, and immediately on my return went inland. When I came down to Ticao again I began to hear queer little rumors. There was an undercurrent of uneasiness everywhere. The Dona Clotilde had been stirring things up. She had called together the wives of the traders at one of her teas — or whatever they were — and made remarks that were distinctly revolutionary. I think she hoped to start petticoat politics in Ticao. The traders' wives, however, told their husbands about the Dona Clotilde's ideas. Their husbands told the Governor. The Dona Clotilde was informed she must not meddle.

There was a second warning for the Governor to send her back to Portugal. He still did not heed it. The ancient city of Ticao had been gentle with him, as it was later gentle with the Dona Clotilde. She was bored. She had no society, little opportunity to play the Governor's wife, and very much leisure. Lobara, her brown-skinned maid, enlightened her to many customs of the city. Lobara was deep in her affair with the huge cook, but her deposition from her former rank still vexed her. Before the arrival of the Dona Clotilde she had been unofficial head of the household. Now, she was a mere domestic servant. Before, she had power over all the other slaves. Now, she was one of them. She naturally hated the Dona Clotilde.

I really think that her only object, at first, was to secure better quarters, better food, and more liberty for herself. She began to tell the Dona Clotilde harrowing tales of the hardships of the slaves. She expatiated upon the suffering of the blacks torn from their homes and families, marched for many months down toward the coast, perhaps dying by the roadside, and to reach as the end of it all simply a heart-breaking, never ending labor under cruel overseers. All she said in this line was probably true. I do not think it would be easy to exaggerate the amount of human misery caused by the slave trade in Ticao, under its farcical disguise of a contract labor system. At the same time, however, it would seem a little odd for a slave to spend an endless amount of ingenuity in convincing one of the slave-owning class that slavery should be abolished. One would expect a slave, rather, to devote his or her time to flattering the white man in hopes of having the slave's condition improved as a reward. Lobara did not do that, though. Considering her later actions, I have never been quite able to decide whether she foresaw what the result of her constant tales would be and was carrying out an involved and intricate plan, or whether she was simply trying to work upon the Dona Clotilde's sympathies to secure better conditions for herself.

She told about a certain trader up near the Hungry Country who had opened a rum store. A native worker from one of the missions had Christianized one of the native villages nearby, and the natives did not buy rum from him. The trader was extremely angry, accused the missionaries of interfering with trade, complained to the Governor, and received ample powers to enforce his will. Now, practically all of the inhabitants of that village are *servaçaes*, and the remainder are drink-sodden objects who are gradually being seized for their debts to the trader. Lobara likewise gave exact and intimate details of the march of Silva Porto's caravan of slaves. He has brought out very many slaves from the interior, and for all I know may still be bringing them, but the case Lobara mentioned is one everyone knew of. He had nine hundred slaves six weeks' march back from the Hungry Country. He brought them down to the coast. Three hundred of them lived to reach Ticao. There was another story. A trader in Ticao — his name was da Cunha — found ground glass in his food. It isn't extremely uncommon. Slaves will try to poison their masters when they're badly treated, and da Cunha was on the lookout. Da Cunha thought it was his cook and made no inquiry; he simply beat the man to death with a hippo whip. Later on it turned out that the guilty party was another of his native boys. Da Cunha shot the other one, and in course of time the story leaked out. Everyone agreed that he was perfectly right in shooting the real culprit, but it was thought that he should have made an investigation and made sure he was beating the right one to death. Da Cunha was punished by being ordered to leave Ticao for three months. He spent the time in Mozambique, furiously angry with the Governor. That had been some time ago, however, and the Governor in question was not the Dona Clotilde's husband.

As I said, the Dona Clotilde had an imperious mouth. She had a great deal of energy. When Lobara worked upon her feelings, the Dona Clotilde decided that something should be done. Now, one of the traditions of the city of Ticao is that nothing shall be done that will alter the scheme of things as they are. Here was the first attempt of the Dona Clotilde to violate those traditions. The city reproached her gently through her husband. She had gone to him to beg him to do something to alleviate the slavery of the blacks. Merely to require the whites to fulfill the terms of their contracts would be a blessing to the slaves. To be released at the end of four years would in itself do much to redeem the slaves from their stupor of despair.

The Governor was furious with her. She had not been long in the Ticaoan climate, and she did not understand the unholy things the heat does to a man's nerves and temper. Instead of tolerantly putting his rage down to those causes or to "liver," the Dona Clotilde felt herself insulted, and withdrew into an icy calm. The Governor puffed himself back into a measure of quietness again, and presently went to her and explained that he had not meant to be so discourteous, but that it was quite impossible to do anything for the blacks. The Dona Clotilde, womanlike, mistook his amends for surrender, and told him that when he had acceded to her desires he might expect to be forgiven for his unpardonable manner and language. The Governor was short and very fat, and his temper would never have been of the best, but in Ticao it was atrocious. He lost it again and, in the heat of the quarrel that instantly began, he told the Dona Clotilde precisely how meddlesome he considered her efforts.

He could not have done more than a very little, anyway. If he antagonized the traders he would soon be removed from office, and the traders would be antagonized by anything that affected their profits. The fact that their profits demanded the perpetuation of a monstrous crime against humanity made no difference. People are very much alike everywhere.

Lobara perceived the wide breach between the Governor and the Dona Clotilde. The Dona Clotilde was furious and icy, the Governor was helpless and infuriated. I don't know whether Lobara had first planned this state of things or not. Probably she was clever enough. Personally, I think that she merely hoped to reduce the Dona Clotilde to a state of maudlin sentimentality in which she would relieve her own slaves from all work and feed them well. That seems to be the only ambition of some of the blacks. When Lobara saw the wide chasm between the Governor and his wife, however, she instantly conceived a wider and better scheme. She would practice her charms upon the Governor again, have the Dona Clotilde sent back to Portugal, and resume her interrupted rule over the Governor's household. She began to work upon that plan at once. Of course she could have no direct communication with the traders' wives, but among the brown-skinned mistresses of the greater number of the whites she spread stories to the effect that the Governor's wife was determined to convert her husband to an anti-slavery policy. The stories reached the traders, of course. Da Cunha waxed immensely indignant.

Lobara next spread a story that the Governor was secretly converted, and only waited an opportunity to harass and impede the slave trade in every possible way. The traders rose up in arms. The slave trade is the only thing that makes Ticao a profitable colony at all. If it were not for the traffic in slaves to the islands the administration expenses of the colony could not possibly be met from its revenues, and assuredly there would be no profits for the traders.

The governmental officials under the Governor himself were no less alarmed at the rumor. Every man who accepts a post in Ticao goes there with the hope of accumulating a competence in the three or four years of his term of office. Naturally, that competence does not come from his pay. And all "extras" are perquisites from the slave trade or the trade in sugar-cane rum which is allied to and a part of the slave trade.

The Dona Clotilde heard of the uproar, and instantly began to consider herself a martyr. If there be any one thing a woman enjoys more than any other, it is the exquisite pleasure of displaying the fortitude and Christian resignation with which she can endure unjust persecution. The Dona Clotilde began to take a fanatical interest in her slaves, merely because she was more or less persecuted for her efforts to relieve them. They became lazy and insolent, as slaves will. If the Dona Clotilde's interest had been sincere, she would have had but little danger from that cause. Blacks are quick to discover hypocrisy, however, and they saw that her interest in them was indulged in merely for the morbid pleasure of being persecuted and of pitying herself for that persecution. They took advantage of the Dona Clotilde's weak lenience.

The Governor grew more irritable as his slaves went unconnected and uncontrolled. The Dona Clotilde went about in a frenzy of shallow, fanatical uplift. Nothing was too good for her slaves, partly to repair the damage they had suffered in being made slaves. Lobara plunged into her affair with the cook, because she saw it would soon be over — the Governor's patience would not last much longer.

The matter came to a calm and carefully deliberated climax. The Governor was informed that the Dona Clotilde by her activities was causing serious unrest among the slaves in Ticao. She would have to be stopped, or some way would be found to have the Governor removed from office. I think the decision came from the directors of the steamship line to the islands, reinforced by the owners of the larger *roças* on San Felipe and by the *sociedades de recrutamente* — the slave trading companies. A conference was held by those people in Lisbon, I was told.

The Governor had the choice between sending his wife home to Portugal, you see, or of losing his position and his generous perquisites. His wife was still an iceberg to him, and she was thoroughly disorganizing his household. He told her she would have to go home to Portugal.

Manners are not much insisted upon in Ticao as a rule, but Portuguese are white people, in the last analysis, and therefore cannot be frank even with themselves. Everyone in all Ticao knew what was the real cause of the Dona Clotilde's return, but we were told officially that ill health made it necessary that the Dona Clotilde go to Portugal to recuperate. We all called at the governmental palace to express our regret — all but da Cunha. There was something uncivilized about that man which made him more honest than the rest of us. At that time he was carrying about in a little phial attached to his watch-chain the ground glass that had been put in his food by one of his slaves. He alone did not express his regret that the Dona Clotilde was leaving Ticao, but he went to the last official dinner before she left.

You people who live in settled, orderly communities know how gossip travels. You know that your wives can tell you most intimate details of the lives of your neighbors, and you have more than a suspicion that your lives are equally well known to them. That is in a civilized, cultured place. In Ticao gossip is swifter and more complete. Nearly every white man in the city had learned that Lobara had been restored to her former position even before the Dona Clotilde left. The news restored confidence in the Governor and relieved the traders' apprehension that some leaven of the Dona Clotilde's anti-slavery ideas might still be working in her husband's mind. If he had restored Lobara to her place in his affections, all was well.

The boat that went up the coast, past the islands and to the steamer-port for Lisbon, was due to arrive on the next day.

A farewell banquet at the Governor's palace was to be given the Dona Clotilde. The Governor, short and fat, sat at the head of the table, and drank heavily. The Dona Clotilde, pale and blazing defiance at all of us, sat beside him. Military officers of the colony came, resplendent in slightly tarnished gold lace. They drank heavily. Traders came. The traders' wives came. All the world — all the wholly white Ticaoan world — came; to the farewell banquet in the state dining room of the Governor's palace. The room was dusty and moldy. The flickering light in the dusty crystal chandelier above shone on a pitiful attempt at splendor. The room was large and had once been magnificent, but that was in the days of Ticao's glory. When slave ships waited for their living freight, when Ticao was the center of a thriving trade in human flesh, when Brazilian coffee had not captured the market and Ticao produced great quantities of that article for the world, when the Cathedral of Our Lady of Mercy was the scene of impressive ecclesiastical ceremonies — when Ticao was in its glory, the court of the Governor of Ticao was a brilliant sight. Now the colony ships a few thousand slaves a year to the islands. The natives are growing so scarce that enough cannot be found to operate the *roças* of San Felipe and Gomé as they should be operated. Now Ticao is an old and decaying but beautiful town which preserves its traditions unchanged. Now the Governor's palace is damp and moldy. Now the Governor's court is a dismal thing of rapacious traders and sallow traders' wives where once were brilliant officers and learned priests, of a dozen or two-dozen slaves where there were once hundreds, of cheap drinks compounded of gin and limes where once the rarest vintages flowed.

Not quite comprehending the whole affair, I was yet somehow impressed by the triumphant air of a slave woman who did not serve us, but stood in one of the doorways of the huge dining room and looked in. She was better dressed than a slave usually is dressed, and wore a gaudy comb in her hair. I had heard enough to know it must be Lobara, restored to her former position as the Governor's favorite. As I glanced at the doorway a black face appeared over her shoulder. She turned to the man and spoke impatiently, her eyes flashing. Uncontrollable rage flashed over the male slave's features. He stared into the dining room and his expression flared into malicious triumph. Instinctively, my eyes followed his. The Governor was just lifting a forkful of an especially succulent fish to his mouth.

At just that moment, da Cunha suddenly spat out what food was in his mouth, the first mouthful of fish. He rose to his feet. A squat revolver glistened in his hand.

"Excellency," he said with deadly quietness, "this food is poisoned. Hadn't you better call your cook?"

You see? Lobara, on being restored to the Governor's favor, had discarded her slave love — the cook. Spoiled by the Dona Clotilde's lenience, he went about raging. At last, when the Dona Clotilde was to leave Ticao and Lobara was to resume her former place of importance in the Governor's household, his jealous rage got the better of him and he had attempted to poison the Governor, It meant poisoning the rest of us too, but that was a detail he ignored.

Few of us had eaten much of the fish, however, so we were able to take precautions at once. The Dona Clotilde was sick, and could not take the steamer she intended. When she had recovered, her feelings toward the blacks had altered so much that there was no objection to her remaining in Ticao. The cook was flogged to death and Lobara was sold to San Felipe. The Governor had had enough of a fright to keep him faithful to the Dona Clotilde ever after, and the Dona Clotilde was at last convinced that slavery, and abject slavery, was the only possible estate for the blacks. She had attempted to ease their lot, and had been poisoned for her pains. When she recovered her strength her slaves soon learned of her change of attitude. In Ticao nowadays they say that the Governor's slaves are fed some meal, some dried fish, and a great deal of *chiboka*. A *chiboka* is the favorite whip used by slave traders in "taming" their slaves.

As I said, the city of Ticao is very old, and very beautiful, it; has that indefinable quality of atmosphere, which means that it has traditions which must be lived up to. In Ticao you must do as the Ticaoans do, or the city and all the generations at its back will see that you suffer for your temerity. Consider the case of the Dona Clotilde!

MORALE

A Story of the War of 1941–43

PART I

". . . The profound influence of civilian morale upon the course of modern war is nowhere more clearly shown than in the case of that monstrous war-engine popularly known as a 'Wabbly.' It landed in New Jersey Aug. 16, 1942, and threw the whole Eastern Coast into a frenzy. In six hours the population of three States was in a panic. Industry was paralyzed. The military effect was comparable only to a huge modern army landed in our rear. . . ." (*Strategic Lessons of the War of 1941–43.* — U. S. War College. Pp. 79–80.)

Sergeant Walpole made his daily report at 2:15. He used a dinky telephone that should have been in a museum, and a rural Central put him on the Area Officer's tight beam. The Area Officer listened drearily as the Sergeant said in a military manner:

"Sergeant Walpole, sir, Post Fourteen, reports that he has nothing of importance to report."

The Area Officer's acknowledgment was curt; embittered. For he was an energetic young man, and he loathed his job. He wanted to be in the west, where fighting of a highly unconventional nature was taking place daily. He did not enjoy this business of watching an unthreatened coast-line simply for the maintenance of civilian confidence and morale. He preferred fighting.

Sergeant Walpole, though, exhaled a lungful of smoke at the telephone transmitter and waited. Presently the rural Central said:

"All through?"

"Sure, sweetie," said Sergeant Walpole. "How about the talkies tonight?"

That was at 2:20 P.M. There was coy conversation, while the civilian telephone-service suffered. Then Sergeant Walpole went back to his post of duty with a date for the evening. He never kept that date, as it turned out. The rural Central was dead an hour after the first and only Wabbly landed, and as everybody knows, that happened at 2:45.

But Sergeant Walpole had no premonitions as he went back to his hammock on the porch. This was Post Number Fourteen, Sixth Area, Eastern Coast Observation Force. There was a war on, to be sure. There had been a war on since the fall of 1941, but it was two thousand miles away. Even lone-wolf bombing planes, flying forty thousand feet up, never came this far to drop their eggs upon inviting targets or upon those utterly blank, innocent-seeming places where munitions of war were now manufactured underground.

Here was peace and quiet and good rations and a paradise for gold-brickers. Here was a summer bungalow taken over for military purposes, quartering six men who watched a certain section of coast-line for a quite impossible enemy. Three miles to the south there was another post. Three miles to the north another one still. They stretched all along the Atlantic Coast, those observation-posts, and the men in them watched the sea, languidly observed the television broadcasts, and slept in the sun. That was all they were supposed to do. In doing it they helped to maintain civilian morale. And therefore the Eastern Coast Observation Force was enviously said to be "just attached to the Army for rations," by the other services, and its members rated with M.P.'s and other low forms of animal life.

Sergeant Walpole reclined in his hammock, inhaling comfortably. The ocean glittered blue before him in the sun. There was a plume of smoke out at sea indicating an old-style coal-burner, its hull down below the horizon. Anything that would float was being used since the war began, though a coal-burning ship was almost a museum piece. A trim Diesel tramp was lazing northward well inshore. A pack of gulls were squabbling noisily over some unpleasantness floating a hundred yards from the beach. The Diesel tramp edged closer inshore still. It was all very peaceful and placid. There are few softer jobs on earth than being a member of a "force in being" for the sake of civilian morale.

But at 2:32 P.M. the softness of that job departed, as far as Sergeant Walpole was concerned. At that moment he heard a thin wailing sound high aloft. It was well enough known nearer the front, but the Eastern Coast Observation Force had had no need to become unduly familiar with it. With incredible swiftness the wailing rose to the shrillest of shrieks, descending as lightning might be imagined to descend. Then there was a shattering concussion. It was monstrous. It was ear-splitting. Windows crashed in the cottage and tinkled to the sandy earth outside. There was a pause of seconds' duration only, during which Sergeant Walpole stared blankly and gasped, "What the hell?" Then there was a second thin wailing which rose to a scream. . . .

Sergeant Walpole was in motion before the second explosion

came. He was diving off the veranda of Post Number Fourteen. He saw someone else coming through a window. He had a photographic glimpse of one of his men emerging through a doorway. Then he struck earth and began to run. Like everybody else in America, he knew what the explosions and the screamings meant.

But he had covered no more than fifty yards when the third bomb fell from that plane so far aloft that it was not even a mote in the sky. Up there the sky was not even blue, but a dull leaden gray because of the thinness of the atmosphere yet above it. The men in that high-flight bomber could see the ground only as a mass of vaguely blending colors. They were aiming their bombs by filtered light, through telescopes which used infra-red rays only, as aerial cameras did back in the 1920s. And they were sighting their eggs with beautifully exact knowledge of their velocity and height. By the time the bombs had dropped eight miles they were traveling faster than the sound of their coming. The first two had wiped out Posts Thirteen and Fifteen. The third made no sound before it landed, except to an observer at a distance. Sergeant Walpole heard neither the scream of fall nor the sound of its explosion.

He was running madly, and suddenly the earth bucked violently beneath his feet, and he had a momentary sensation of things flying madly by over his head, and then he knew nothing at all for a very long time. Then his head ached horribly and someone was popping at something valorously with a rifle, and he heard the nasty sharp explosions of the hexynitrate bullets which have remodeled older ideas of warfare, and Sergeant Walpole was aware of an urgent necessity to do something, but he could not at all imagine what it was. Then a shell went off, the earth-concussion banged his nose against the sand, and the rifle-fire stopped.

"For Gawd's sake!" said Sergeant Walpole dizzily.

He staggered to his feet and looked behind him. Where the cottage had been there was a hole. Quite a large hole. It was probably a hundred yards across and all of twenty deep, but sea-water was seeping in to fill it through the sand. Its edge was forty or fifty feet from where he stood. He had been knocked down by the heaving earth, and the sand and mud blown out of the crater had gone clean over him. Twenty feet back, the top part of his body would have been cut neatly off by the blast. As it was. . . .

He found his nose bleeding and plugged it with his handkerchief. He was still rather dazed, and he still had the feeling that there was something extremely important that he must do. He stood rocking on his feet, trying to clear his head, when two men came along the sand-dunes behind the beach. One of them carried two automatic rifles. The other was trying to bandage a limp and flapping arm as he ran. They saw the Sergeant and ran to him.

"Hell, Sarge, I thought y'were blown to little egg-shells."

"I ain't," said Sergeant Walpole. He looked again at the hole in the ground and swore painedly.

"Look at that," said the man with the flapping arm. "Hell's goin' to pop around here, Sarge."

The sergeant swung around. Then his mouth dropped open. Just half a mile away and hardly more than two hundred yards from the shore-line, the Diesel tramp was ramming the beach. A wake still foamed behind it. A monstrous bow-wave spread out on either hand, over-topping even the combers that came rolling in. It was being deliberately run ashore. It struck, and its fore-mast crumpled up and fell forward, carrying its derrick-booms with it. There was the squeal of crumpled metal plates.

"Flyin' a yeller flag just now," panted one of the two privates. "We started poppin' hexynitrate bullets at her an' she flung a shell at us. She's a enemy ship. But what the hell?"

Smoke spurted up from the beached ship. Her stern broke off and settled in the deeper water out from the shore. More smoke spurted out. Her bow split wide. There were the deep rumbles of black-powder explosions. Sergeant Walpole and his two followers stared blankly. More explosions, and the ship was hidden in smoke, and when it blew away her funnel was down and half or more of her upper works was sliding into the sea, and she had listed suddenly.

Sergeant Walpole gazed upward. Futilely, of course; there was nothing in sight overhead. But these explosions did look like the hexynitrate stuff they put in small-arm bullets nowadays. A thirty-caliber bullet had the explosive effect of an old-style six-pound T.N.T. shell. Only, hexynitrate goes off with a crack instead of a boom. It wasn't an American plane opening up with a machine-gun.

Then the beached ship seemed to blow up. A mass of thick smoke covered her from stem to stern, and bits of plating flew heavily through the air, and there were a few lurid bursts of flame. Sergeant Walpole suddenly remembered that there ought to be survivors, only he hadn't seen anybody diving overboard to try to get ashore. He half-started forward. . . .

Then the sea-breeze blew this smoke, too, away from the

wreckage. And the tramp was gone, but there was something else left in its place — so that Sergeant Walpole took one look, and swallowed a non-existent something that came up instantly into his throat again, and remembered the urgent thing he had to do.

"Pete," he said calmly, "you hunt up the Area Officer an' tell him what you seen. Here! I'll give you a report that'll keep 'em from slammin' you in clink for bein' drunk. Grab a monocycle somewheres. It's faster than a car, the way you'll be travelin'. First telephone you come to that's workin', make Central put you in the tight beam to head-quarters. Then go on an' report, y'self. See?"

Pete started, and automatically fumbled with his limp and useless arm. Then he carefully tucked the unmanageable hand in the pocket of his uniform blouse.

"That don't matter now," he said absurdly.

He was looking at the thing left in place of the tramp, as Sergeant Walpole scribbled on one of the regulation report-forms of the Eastern Coast Observation Force. And the thing he saw was enough to upset anybody.

Where the tramp had been there was a single bit of bow-plating sticking up out of the surf, and a bunch of miscellaneous floating wreckage drifting sluggishly toward the beach. And there was a solid, rounded, metallic shape apparently quite as long as the original tramp had been. There was a huge armored tube across its upper part, with vision-slits in two bulbous sections at its end. There were gun-ports visible here and there, and already a monstrous protuberance was coming into view midway along its back, as if forced into position from within. Where the bow of the tramp had been there were colossal treads now visible. There was a sort of conning-tower, armored and grim. There was a ghastly steel beak. The thing was a war-machine of monstrous size. It emitted a sudden roaring sound, as of internal-combustion engines operating at full power, and lurched heavily. The steel plates of the tramp still visible above water, crumpled up like paper and were trodden under. The thing came toward the shore. It slithered through the shallow sea, with waves breaking against its bulging sides. It came out upon the beach, its wet sides glittering. It was two hundred feet long, and it looked somehow like a gigantic centipede.

It was a tank, of sorts, but like no tank ever seen on earth before. It was the great-grandfather of all tanks. It was so monstrous that for its conveyance a ship's hull and superstructure had been built about it, and its own engines had been the engines of that ship. It was so huge that it could only be landed by blasting away a beached ship from about itself, so it could run under its own power over the fragments to the shore.

Now it stopped smoothly on the sandy beach, in which its eight-foot-wide steel treads sank almost a yard. Men dropped down from ports in its swelling sides. They made swift, careful inspections of predetermined points. They darted back up the ladders again. The thing roared once more. Then it swung about, headed for the sand-dunes, and with an extraordinary smoothness and celerity disappeared inland.

PART II

"... The Wabbly was meant for one purpose, the undermining of civilian morale. To accomplish that purpose it set systematically about the establishment of a reign of terror; and so complete was its success that half the population of a state was in headlong flight within two hours. It was, first, mysterious; secondly, deadly, and within a very few hours it had built up a reputation for invincibility. Judged on the basis of its first twelve hours' work alone, it was the most successful experiment of the war. Its effect on civilian morale was incalculable." (*Strategic Lessons of the War of 1941–43.* — U. S. War College. Pp. 80–81.)

Two of the members of Observation-Post Fourteen gaped after the retreating monster. Sergeant Walpole scribbled on the official form. Just as the monstrous thing dipped down out of sight there was a vicious, crashing report from its hinder part. Something shrieked. . . .

Sergeant Walpole got up, spitting sand. There was blood on the report-form in his hand. He folded it painstakingly. Of the two men who had been with him, one was struggling out of the sand as Sergeant Walpole had had to do. The other was scattered over a good many square yards of sandy beach.

"Um. They seen us," said Sergeant Walpole, "an' they got Pete. You'll have to take this report. I'm goin' after the damn thing."

"What for?" asked the other man blankly.

"To keep it in sight," said Sergeant Walpole. "That's tactics. If somebody springs somethin' you ain't able to fight, run away but keep it in sight an' report to the nearest commissioned officer. Remember that. Now get on. There's monocycles in the village. Get there an' beat that damn Wabbly thing with the news."

He saw his follower start off, sprinting. That particular soldier, by the way, was identified by his dog-tag some days later. As nearly as could be discovered, he had died of gas. But Sergeant Walpole picked up one of the two rifles, blew sand out of the breech-mechanism, and started off after the metal monster. He walked in the eight-foot track of one of its treads. As he went, he continued the cleaning of sand from the rifle in his hands. The rifle was useless against such a monster, of course, but it is quaint to reflect that in that automatic rifle, firing hexynitrate bullets, each equivalent to a six-pounder T.N.T. shell in destructiveness, Sergeant Walpole carried greater "fire-power" than Napoleon ever disposed in battle.

The tread of the Wabbly made a perfect roadway. Presently Sergeant Walpole looked up to find himself scrutinizing somebody's dining-room table, set for lunch. The Wabbly had crossed a house in its path without swerving. Walls, chimneys, timbers and planks, all had gone beneath its treads. But they had been pressed so smoothly flat that until Sergeant Walpole looked down at his footing, he would not have known he was walking on the wreckage of a building.

It was half an hour before he reached the village. The Wabbly had gone from end to end, backed up, and gone over the rest of it again. There was the taint of gas in the air. Sergeant Walpole halted outside the debris. His gas-mask had been blown to atoms with Observation-Post Fourteen.

"They're tryin' to beat the news o' their comin'," he reflected aloud, "which is why they smashed up the village. The telephone exchange was there. . . . Tillie's under there somewheres. . . ."

He fumbled with the rifle, suddenly swearing queerly hate-distorted oaths. Tillie had not been the great love of Sergeant Walpole's life. She was merely a country telephone operator, reasonably pretty, and flattered by his uniform. But she was under a mass of splintered wood and crushed brick-work, killed while trying to connect with the tight beam to Area Headquarters to report the monster rushing upon the village. That monster had destroyed the little settlement. There was nothing left at all but wreckage and the eight-foot tracks of monster treads. Sometimes those tracks crossed each other. Between them wreckage survived to a height of as much as four feet, which was the clearance of the Wabbly's body.

Something roared low overhead. Sergeant Walpole swore bitterly, looked upward, and waited to die. But the small plane was American, and old. It was a training-plane, useless for front-line work. It dived to earth, the pilot waved impatiently, and Walpole plunged to a place beside him. Instantly thereafter the plane took off.

"What was it?" shouted the pilot, sliding off at panic-stricken speed across the tree-tops. "They heard the bombs go off all the way to Philly. Sent me. What in hell was it?"

A thin, high, wailing sound coming down as lightning might be imagined to descend. . . . The pilot dived madly and got behind a pine forest before the explosion and the concussion that followed it. Sergeant Walpole saw the pine-trees shiver. The sheer explosion-wave of that egg, if it hit an old ship like this in mid-air, would have stripped the fabric from its wings.

"Set me down," said Sergeant Walpole. "They're watchin' us from aloft. I sent a man on a monocycle to report." But he told luridly of the thing that had come ashore, and of its destructiveness. "Now set me down. Gimme a gas-mask an' clear out. You ain't got a burglar's chance of gettin' back."

The pilot set him down, and began ticking away on a code sender even as he landed. Then he climbed swiftly away from the Sergeant, headed in a weaving, crazy line to westward. Then things screamed downward and the Sergeant clapped hands over his ears once more. The ground quivered underfoot, though the eggs landed a good three-quarters of a mile away. The training-plane dropped like a plummet. The sharpness of a hexynitrate explosion carries its effect to quite incredible distances. The fabric of its wings split to ribbons. The ship landed somewhere and smoke rose from it.

"He shouldn't ha' gone up so high," said Sergeant Walpole.

He struck across country for the treads of the Wabbly once more. He saw a school-house. The Wabbly had passed within a hundred yards of it. The school-house seemed deserted. Then the Sergeant saw the hole in its roof. Then he caught the infinitely faint taint of gas.

"Mighty anxious," said Sergeant Walpole woodenly, "not to let news get ahead of 'em. Yeah. . . . If it busts on places without warnin', it'll have that much easier work. I hope I'm in on the party when we get this damn thing."

There was no use in approaching the school-house, though he had a gas-mask now. Sergeant Walpole went on.

PART III

"... The Wabbly made no attempt to do purely military damage. The Enemy command realized that the destruction of civilian morale was even more important than the destruction of munitions factories. In this, the Enemy displayed the same acumen that makes the war a fruitful subject of study to the strategic student." (*Strategic Lessons of the War of 1941–43.* — U. S. War College. Pp. 81–82.)

At nightfall the monster swerved suddenly and moved with greater speed. It showed no lights. It did not even make very much noise. Then the second flight of home-defense planes made their attack. Sergeant Walpole heard them droning overhead. He lit a fire instantly. A little helicopter dropped from the blackness above him and he began to heap dirt desperately on the blaze.

"Who's there?" demanded a voice.

"Sergeant Walpole, Post Fourteen, Eastern Coast Observation," said the Sergeant in a military manner. "Beg to report, sir, that the dinkus that brought down the other ships is housed in that big bulge on top of the Wabbly."

"Get in," said the voice.

The Sergeant obeyed. With a purring noise the helicopter shot upward. Then something went off in mid-sky, miles ahead, where a faint humming noise had announced the flight of attack-planes. A lurid, crackling detonation lit up the sky. One of the ships of the night-flying squadron. From the helicopter they could see the rest of the flight limned clearly in the flash of the explosion. Instantly thereafter there was another such flash. Then another.

"Three," said the voice beside Sergeant Walpole. Another flash. "Four. . . ." The invisible operator of the screw-lifted ship was very calm about it. "Five. Six." The explosions lit the sky. Presently he said grimly. "That's all of them. I'd better report it."

He was silent for a while. Sergeant Walpole saw his hand flicking a key up and down in the faint light of radio bulbs.

"Now shoot the works," said the helicopter man evenly. "All the ships that attacked this afternoon went down. One of them started to report, but didn't get but two words through. What did that damned thing use on them?"

"A dinkus on top, sir," said Sergeant Walpole formally. "I'd found a monocycle, sir, and was trailing the thing. I'd come to the top of a hill and seen it moving through a pine-wood, crashing down the trees in front of it like they wasn't there. Then a egg came down from Gawd-knows-where up aloft. I stopped up my ears, thinkin' it was aimin' for me. Then I seen the ships. Two of 'em were fallin'. They landed, an' I heard a coupla other explosions. Little ones, they sounded like."

The helicopter man's wrist was flicking up and down.

"Little ones!" he said sardonically. "Those ships were carrying five-hundred-pound bombs! It was those you heard going off!"

"Maybe," conceded Sergeant Walpole. "There was twenty or thirty ships flyin' in formation, goin' hell-for-leather for the Wabbly. They were trailin' it from the air. They were comin', natural, for me, because I was between them an' it. Then my pants caught on fire —"

"What?"

"My pants caught on fire," said Sergeant Walpole, woodenly. "I was sittin' on the monocycle, tryin' to figure out which way to duck. An' my pants caught on fire. The bike was gettin' hot. I climbed off it an' it blew up. My rifle was hot, too, an' I chucked it away. Then I saw a ship go down, on fire. The Wabbly'd stopped still an' it didn't fire a shot. I'll swear to that. Just my monocycle got hot an' caught on fire, an' then a ship busted out in flames an' went down. A couple more eggs come down an' three ships dropped. Didn't hit 'em. The concussion blew the fabric off 'em. Another one caught fire an' crashed. Then another one. I looked, an' saw the next one catch. Then the next. It was like a searchlight beam hittin' 'em. They flamed up, blew up, an' that was that. The last two tried to get away, but they lit up an' crashed."

The pilot's hand flicked up and down, interminably. There was the steady fierce down-beat of the slip-stream from the vertical propellers. The helicopter swept forward in a swooping dash.

"The whole east coast's gone crazy," said the 'copter man drily. "Crazy fools trying to run away. Roads jammed. Work stopped. It leaked out about the planes being wiped out to-day, and everybody in three states has heard those eggs going off. You're the only living man who's seen that crawling thing and lived to tell about it. I've sent your stuff back. What's that about the thing on top?"

"I hid," said Sergeant Walpole, woodenly. "The Wabbly sent over gas-shells where the ships landed. Then it went on. Headin' west. It's got a crazy-lookin' dinkus on top like a searchlight. That moved, while the ships were catchin' fire an' crashin'. Just like a searchlight, it moved an' the ships went down. But the Wabbly didn't fire a shot."

The helicopter man's wrist flexed swiftly. . . .

"Gawd!" said Sergeant Walpole in sudden agony. "Drop! Quick!"

The helicopter went down like a stone. A propeller shrieked

away into space. Metalwork up aloft glowed dully red. Then there were whipping, lashing branches closing swiftly all around the helicopter. A jerk. A crash. Stillness. The smell of growing things all about.

"Well?" said the 'copter pilot.

"They turned it on us — whatever it is," said Sergeant Walpole. "They near got us, too."

A match scratched. A cigarette glowed. The Sergeant fumbled for a smoke for himself.

"I'm waiting for that metal to cool off," said the helicopter pilot. "Maybe we can take off again. They located us with a loop while I was sending your stuff. Damn! I see what they've got!"

"What?"

"A way of transmitting real power in a radio beam," said the 'copter man. "You've seen eddy-current stoves. Everybody cooks with 'em nowadays. A coil with a high-frequency current. You can stick your hand in it and nothing happens. But you stick an iron pan down in the coil and it gets hot and cooks things. Hysteresis. The same thing that used to make transformer-cores get hot. The same thing happens near any beam transmitter, only you have to measure the heating effect with a thermo-couple. The iron absorbs the radio waves and gets hot. The chaps in the Wabbly can probably put ten thousand horsepower in a damned beam. We can't. But any iron in the way will get hot. It blows up a ship at once. Your monocycle and your rifle too. Damn!"

He knocked the ash off his cigarette.

"Scientific, those chaps. I'll see if that metal's cool."

Something whined overhead, rising swiftly to a shriek as it descended. Sergeant Walpole cowered, with his hands to his ears. But it was not an earth-shaking concussion. It was an explosion, yes, but subtly different from the rending snap of hexynitrate.

"Gas," said the Sergeant dully, and fumbled for his mask.

"No good," said the 'copter man briefly. "Vesicatory. Smell it? I guess they've got us. No sag-suits. Not even sag-paste."

The Sergeant lit a match. The flame bent a little from the vertical.

"There's a wind. We got a chance."

"Get going, then," said the 'copter man. "Run upwind."

Sergeant Walpole slid over the side and ran. A hundred yards. Two hundred. Pine-woods have little undergrowth. He heard the helicopter's engines start. The ship tried to lift. He redoubled his speed. Presently he broke out into open ploughed land.

In the starlight he saw a barn, and he raced toward that. Someone else plunged out of the woods toward him. The helicopter-engine was still roaring faintly in the distance. Then a thin whine came down from aloft. . . .

When the echoes of the explosion died away the pilot was grinning queerly. The helicopter's engine was still.

"I said it could be done! Pack of fat-heads at Headquarters!"

"Huh?"

"Picking up a ship by its spark-plugs, with a loop. They're doing that up aloft. There's a ship up there, forty thousand feet or so. Maybe half a dozen ships. Refueling in air, I guess, and working with the thing you call a Wabbly. When I started the 'copter's engine they got the spark-impulses and sighted on them. We'd better get away from here."

"Horses in here," said Sergeant Walpole. "The Wabbly came by. No people left."

They brought the animals out. The horses reared and plunged as there were other infinitely sharp, deadly explosions of the eggs coming down eight miles through darkness.

"Let's go. After the Wabbly?" said the 'copter man.

"O' course," said Sergeant Walpole. "Somebody's got to find out how to lick it."

They went clattering through darkness. It was extraordinary what desolation, what utter lack of human life they moved through. They came to a town, and there was a taint of gas in the air. No lights burned in that town. It was dead. The Wabbly had killed it.

PART IV

". . . which panic was enhanced by the destruction of a second flight of fighting planes. However, the destruction of Bendsboro completed civilian demoralization. . . . A newscasting company re-broadcast a private television contact with the town at the moment the Wabbly entered it. Practically all the inhabitants of the Atlantic Coast heard and saw the annihilation of the town — hearing the cries of '*Gas!*' and the screams of the people, and hearing the crashings as the Wabbly crushed its way inexorably across the city, spreading terror everywhere. . . . Frenzied demands were made upon the Government for the recall of troops from the front to offer battle to the Wabbly. . . . It is considered that at that time the one Wabbly had a military effect equal to at least half a million men." (*Strategic Lessons of the War of 1941-43.* — U. S. War College. Pp. 83–84.)

They did not enter the town. There was just enough of starlight to show that the Wabbly had gone through it, and then crashed back and forth ruthlessly. There was a great gash through the center of the buildings nearest the edge, and there were other gashes visible here and there. Everything was crushed down utterly flat in two eight-foot paths; and there was a mass of crumbled debris four feet high at its highest in between the tread-marks.

They looked, silently, and went on. They reached a railroad track, the quadruple track of a branch-line from New York to Philadelphia. The Wabbly was going along that right-of-way. There was no right-of-way left where it had been. Rails were crushed flat. Culverts were broken through. But the horses raced along the smoothed tread-trails. Once a broken, twisted rail tore at Sergeant Walpole's sleeve. Somehow the last great plate of a tread had bent it upward. Presently they saw a mass of something dark off to the left. Flames were licking meditatively at one of the wrecked cars.

Then they heard explosions far ahead. Flames lighted the sky.

"Our men in action!" said Sergeant Walpole hungrily.

He flogged his mount mercilessly. Then the sky became bright in the distance. The horses, going down the crushed-smooth trail of the treads, gained upon the din. Then they saw the cause of it, miles distant. A train was burning luridly. Its forepart was wreckage, pure and simple. The rest was going up in flames and detonations. Munitions, of course. The Wabbly was off at one side, flame-lit and monstrous, sliding smoothly out of sight.

"Ten miles of railroad," said the 'copter pilot calmly, "mashed out of existence. That's going to scare our people into fits. They can drop eggs till the cows come home, and every egg'll smash up a hundred yards of right-of-way, and we can build it back up again in four hours with mobile track-layers. But ten miles to be regraded and laid is different. Half of America will be imagining all our railroads smashed and starvation ahead."

A piercing light fell upon them.

"Shut it off!" roared Sergeant Walpole. "D'y'want to get us killed?"

He and the 'copter pilot swerved. There was a car there, a huge two-wheeled car, whose gyroscopes hummed softly while its driver tried to extract it from something it was tangled in.

"I commandeer this car," said the 'copter pilot. "Military necessity. We have to trail that Wabbly."

Someone grunted. Lights flashed on within. The 'copter pilot and Sergeant Walpole stiffened to attention. The stars of a major-general shone on the collar of the stout man within.

"Beg pardon, sir," said the pilot, and was still.

"Umph," said the major-general. "There seem to be just four of us alive, who've seen the thing clearly. I hit on it by accident, I'll admit. What do you know about it?"

"It come on a tramp-steamer —" began Sergeant Walpole.

"Hm. You're Sergeant Walpole. Mentioned in dispatches to-morrow, Sergeant. You, sir?"

"Its weapon against our planes, sir," said the 'copter man precisely, "is a radio beam carrying several thousand horsepower of energy. When it hits iron, sir, the energy is absorbed and the iron heats up and blows up the ship. The Wabbly's working with a bomber well aloft, sir, which spots planes from below by picking up their spark-plug flashes in a directional loop. The bomber aloft, sir, drops eggs when the Wabbly's attacked. Sergeant Walpole reports several planes disabled by their fabric being blown off their wings."

"I know," said the major-general. "Dammit, the front takes every ship that's fit to go aloft. We have only wrecks back here. You're sure about that spark-plug affair?"

"Yes, sir," said the 'copter pilot. "My ship crashed, sir. I started the motors again, trying to take off. Eggs began to drop about me instantly."

"Nasty!" said the major-general. "I was going to join my men. We've flung a line of artillery ahead of the thing. Motor-driven, of course. But if they can pick up motors by the spark-waves, the bomber knows all about it. Nasty!"

He lit a cigar, calmly. The gyrocar shifted suddenly and backed away from the thing it had been tangled in.

"Why ain't the bombers been shot down?" demanded Sergeant Walpole angrily. "Dammit, sir, if it wasn't for them bombers —"

"Up to an hour ago," said the major-general, "we had lost sixty-eight planes trying to get those bombers. You see, it works both ways. The bombers drop eggs to help the Wabbly defend itself. And the Wabbly uses that power-beam you spoke of to wipe the sky clean about the bombers. I wondered how it was done, before you explained, sir. Do you men want to come with me? Get on the running-board if you like. We shall probably be killed."

The gyrocar purred softly away, with two horses left wandering and two men clinging fast in a sweep of wind. They found a ribbon of concrete road and the wind sang as the car picked up speed. Then, suddenly, it bucked madly and went out of control, and, as suddenly, was passing along the road again. The Wabbly had passed over the roadway here.

And then they heard gunfire ahead. Honest, malevolent gunfire. Flashes lit the horizon. The gyrocar speeded up until it fairly hummed, and the wind rushed into the nostrils and mouths of the men on the running-boards. The cannonade increased. It reached really respectable proportions, until it became a titanic din. As the road rose up a long incline, a shell burst in mid-air in plain view, and the driver of the gyrocar jammed on the brakes and looked down upon the strangest of sights below.

There were other hills yet ahead, and from behind them came that faint, indefinite glow which is the glow of the lights of a city. At the bottom of a valley, a mile and a half distant, there was the Wabbly. Star-shells flared near it, casting it into intolerable brightness and clear relief. And other shells were breaking upon it and all about it. From beyond the rim of hills came the flashes of guns. The air was full of screamings and many crashes.

The Wabbly was motionless. It looked more than ever like a monstrous, deadly centipede. It was under a rain of fire that would have shattered a dreadnaught of the 1920s. Its monstrous treads were motionless. It seemed queerly quiescent, abstracted; it seemed less defiant of the shell-fire that broke upon it like the hail of hell, than indifferent to it. Yes, it seemed indifferent!

Only the queer excrescence on its top moved, and that stirred vaguely. Star-shells floated overhead and bathed it in pitiless light. And it remained motionless. . . . Sergeant Walpole had a vague impression of colossal detonations taking place miles above his head, but the sound was lost in the drumfire of artillery nearer at hand.

Then a gun on the Wabbly moved. It spouted a flash of bluish flame, and then another and another. It seemed to fire gas-shells into the town, at this moment, ignoring the batteries playing upon it. It was still again, while the queer excrescence on its back moved vaguely and shells burst about it in a very inferno.

Then the treads moved, and with a swift celerity the Wabbly moved smoothly forward and up the incline toward the cannonading guns. It went over the top of the incline, and those in the gyrocar saw its reception. Guns opened on it at point-blank range.

Now the Wabbly itself went into action. In the light of star-shells and explosions they saw its guns begin to bellow. It went swiftly and malevolently forward, moving with centipedean smoothness.

It dipped out of sight. The cannonade lessened. Two guns stopped. Three. . . . Half a dozen guns were out of action. A dozen guns ceased to fire. . . . One last weapon boomed desperately at its maximum rate of fire. . . .

That stopped. The night became strangely, terribly still. The major-general put aside his radivision receiver. Though neither the helicopter pilot nor Sergeant Walpole had noticed it, he had opened communication the instant the gyrocar came to a stop. Now the major-general was desperately, terribly white.

"The artillery is wiped out," he observed detachedly. "The Wabbly, it seems, is going on into the town."

They did not want to listen, those men who waited futilely by the gyrocar which had witnessed the invulnerability of the Wabbly to all attack. They did not want to listen at all. But they heard the noises as the Wabbly crashed across the town, and back and forth.

"Morale effect," said the major-general, through stiff lips. "That's what it's for. To break down the morale behind the lines. Good God! What hellish things mere words can mean!"

PART V

". . . The only weak spot in the Wabbly's design, apparently, was the necessity of using its entire engine-power in the power-beam with which it protected itself and its attendant bombers from aerial attack. For a time, before New Brunswick, it was forced to remain still, under fire, while it fought off and destroyed an attacking fleet eight miles above it. With sufficiently powerful artillery, it might have been destroyed at that moment. But it was invulnerable to the artillery available. . . . Deliberately false statements were broadcast to reassure the public, but the public was already skeptical, as it later became incredulous, of official reports of victories. The destruction of New Brunswick became known despite official denials, and colossal riots broke out among the inhabitants of the larger cities, intent upon escape from defenseless towns. . . . Orders were actually issued withdrawing a quarter of a million men from the front-line reserve, with artillery in proportion to their force." (*Strategic Lessons of the War of 1941–43.* — U. S. War College. P. 92.)

The major-general left them at the town, now quite still and silent. Sergeant Walpole said detachedly:

"We'll prob'ly find a portable sender, sir, an' trail the Wabbly. That's about all we can do, sir."

"It looks," said the major-general rather desperately, "as if that is all anybody can do. I'm going on to take command ahead."

The 'copter pilot said politely:

"Sir, if you're going to sow mines for the Wabbly —"

"Of course!"

"That power-beam can explode them, sir, before the Wabbly gets to them. May I suggest, sir, that mine-cases with no metal in them at all would be worth trying?"

"Thank you," said the major-general grimly. "I'll have concrete ones made."

Sergeant Walpole grunted suddenly.

"Look here, sir! The Wabbly stops when it uses that dinkus on top. This guy here says it uses a lotta power — four or five thousan' horsepower."

"More likely ten or twenty," said the 'copter pilot.

"Maybe," said Sergeant Walpole profoundly, "it takes all the power they got to work that dinkus. They were workin' it just now when the artillery was slammin' 'em. So next time you want to tackle it, stick a flock o' bombs around an' attack the bombers too. If they're kept busy down below, maybe the planes can get the bombers, or otherwise they'll get a chance to use a big gun on the Wabbly."

The major-general nodded.

"We four," he observed, "are the only living men who've actually seen the Wabbly and gotten away. I shall use both your suggestions. And I shall not send those orders by radio — not even tight beam radio. I'll carry them myself. Good luck!"

A non-commissioned officer of the Eastern Coast Observation Force and a yet uncommissioned flying cadet waved a cheerful good-by to the major-general in charge of home defense in three states. Then they went on into the town.

"Monocycles first," said Sergeant Walpole. "An' a sender."

The 'copter man nodded. The street-lights of the town dimmed and brightened. The Wabbly had paused only to create havoc, not to produce utter chaos. It had gone back and forth over the town two or three times, spewing out gas as it went. But most of the town was still standing, and the power-house had not been touched. Only its untended Diesels had checked before a fuel-pump cleared.

They found a cycle-shop, its back wall bulged in by wreckage against it. Sergeant Walpole inspected its wares expertly. A voice began to speak suddenly. A television set had somehow been turned on by the crash that bulged the back wall.

"The monster tank has been held in check," said a smug voice encouragingly. "Encountered by home-defense troops and artillery, it proved unable to face shell-fire. . . ."

"Liars!" said the 'copter man calmly. He picked up the nearest loose object and flung it into the bland face of the official news-announcer. The television set went dead, but there were hissings and sputterings in its interior. He had flung a Bissel battery at it, one of a display-group, and its high-tension terminals hissed and sparked among the stray wires in the cabinet.

"That makes me mad," said the 'copter man grimly. "Lying for morale! The other side murders our civilians to break down morale, and our side lies about it to build morale back up again. To hell with morale!"

Sergeant Walpole reached in and pulled out the battery. Bissel batteries turn out six hundred volts these days, and they make a fat spark when short-circuited.

"For Gawd's sake!" said Sergeant Walpole. "If they can pick up sparks from a motor, can't they pick 'em up from this? What the hell y'doin'? Y'want 'em droppin' eggs on us? Say!"

He stopped short, his eyes burning. He began to talk, suddenly groping for words while he waved the high-powered small battery in his hand. The helicopter man listened, at first skeptically and then with an equally hungry enthusiasm.

"Sergeant," he said evenly, "that's an idea! A whale of an idea! A hell of a fine idea! Let's get some rockets!"

"Why rockets?" demanded Sergeant Walpole in his turn. "Whatcha want to do? Celebrate the Fourth o' July?"

The 'copter man explained, this time; and Sergeant Walpole seized upon the addition. Then they began a hunt. They roved the town over, and it was not pleasant. When the Wabbly had gone into that town there had still been very many living human beings in it. Some of them had believed in the ability of the artillery to defend the town against a single monster. Some had had no means of getting away. But all of them had tried to get away when the Wabbly went lurching in among the houses.

For them, the Wabbly had spewed out deadly gases. Also it had simply forged ahead. And the two living men in their gas-masks paid as little attention as possible to the bodies in the streets, most of them in flimsy night-clothing, struck down in frenzied flight, but they could not help seeing too much. . . .

In the end they went back to the artillery-positions and found signal-rockets there. Two full cases of them, marvelously unexploded. A little later two monocycles purred madly in the beaten-down paths of the monstrous treads. Sergeant Walpole bore very many Bissel batteries, which will deliver six hundred volts even on short-circuit for half an hour at a time. The 'copter man carried some of them, too, and both men were loaded down.

When dawn came they were hollow-eyed and gaunt and weary. It had started to rain, too, and both of them were drenched. They could see no more than a couple of hundred yards in every direction, and they were hungry, and they had seen things no man should have to look upon, in the way of destruction. They came upon a wrecked artillery-train just as the world lightened to a pallid gray. Guns twisted and burst. Caissons, no more than shattered scraps of metal, because of the explosion of the shells within them. And the tread-tracks of the Wabbly led across the mess. Steam still rose, hissing softly, from the bent and twisted guns which had burst when they were heated to redness by the power-beam. And there was a staff gyrocar crumpled against a tree where it had been flung by some explosion or other. There were neither sound nor wounded men about; only dead ones. The Wabbly had been here.

"Hullo," said the helicopter man in a dreary levity, "there's a portable vision set in this car. Let's call up the general and see how he is?"

Sergeant Walpole spat. Then he held up his hand. He was listening. Far off in the drumming downpour of the rain there was a rumbling sound. He had heard it before. It was partly made up of the noise of internal-combustion engines of unthinkable power, and partly of grumbling treads forcing a way through reluctant trees. It was a long way off, now, but it was coming nearer.

"The Wabbly," said Sergeant Walpole. "Comin' back. Why? Hell's bells! Why's it comin' back?"

"I don't know," said the 'copter man, "but let's get some rockets fixed up."

The two of them worked almost lackadaisically. They were tired out. But they took the tiny Bissel batteries and twisted the attached wires about the rocket-heads. They had twenty or thirty of them fixed by the time the noise of the Wabbly was very near. There was the noise of felled trees, pushed down by the Wabbly in its progress. Great, crackling crashes, and then crunching sounds, and above them the thunderous smooth purring rumble of the monster. The 'copter man climbed into the upside-down staff car. He turned the vision set on and fiddled absurdly with the controls.

"I'm getting something," he announced suddenly. "The bomber up aloft is sending its stuff down a beam, a tight beam to the Wabbly. Listen to it!"

The uncouth, clacking syllables of the enemy tongue came from the vision set. Someone was speaking crisply and precisely somewhere. Blurred, indistinct flashes appeared on the vision set screen.

"They ought to be worried," the 'copter man said wearily. "Even an infra-red telescope can't pick up a damned thing through clouds like this. And the Wabbly's in a mess without a bomber to help. . . ."

Sergeant Walpole did not reply. He was exhausted. He sat looking tiredly off through the rain in the direction of the approaching noise. Somehow it did not occur to him to run away. He sat quite still, smoking a soggy cigarette.

Something beaked and huge appeared behind a monstrous oak-tree. It came on. The oak-tree crackled, crashed, and went down. It was ground under by the monstrous war-engine that went over it. The Wabbly was unbelievably impersonal and horrible in its progress. There had been a filling-station for gyrocars close by the place where the artillery-train had been wrecked. One of the eight-foot treads loomed over that station, descended upon it — and the filling-station was no more. The Wabbly was then not more than a hundred yards from Sergeant Walpole, less than a city block. He looked at it in a weary detachment. It was as high as a four-story house, and it was two hundred feet long, and forty feet wide at the treads with the monstrous gun-bulges reaching out an extra ten or fifteen feet on either side above. And it came grumbling on toward him.

PART VI

"... Considered as a strategic move, the Wabbly was a triumph. Eighteen hours after its landing, the orders for troops called for half a million men to be withdrawn from the forces at the front and in reserve, and munitions-factories were being diverted from the supply of the front to the manufacture of devices designed to cope with it. This, in turn, entailed changes in the front-line activities of the Command. . . . Altogether, it may be said that the Wabbly, eighteen hours after its landing, was exerting the military pressure of an army of not less than half a million men upon the most vulnerable spot in our defenses — the rear. . . . And when its effect upon civilian morale is considered, the Wabbly, as a force in being, constituted the most formidable military unit in history." (*Strategic Lessons of the War of 1941–43.* — U. S. War College. P. 93.)

As Sergeant Walpole saw the Wabbly, there was no sign of humanity anywhere about the thing. It was a monstrous mass of metal, powder-stained now where shells had burst against it, and it seemed metallically alive, impersonally living. The armored tube with vision-slits at its ends must have been the counterpart of a ship's bridge, but it looked like the eye-ridge of an insect's face. The bulbous control-rooms at the ends looked like a gigantic insect's multi-faceted eyes. And the huge treads, so thick as to constitute armor for their own protection, were so cunningly joined and sprung that they, too, seemed like part of a living thing.

It came within twenty yards of the staff-car with the 'copter man in it and Sergeant Walpole smoking outside. It ignored them. It had destroyed all life at this place. And Sergeant Walpole alone was visible, and he sat motionless and detached, unemotionally waiting to be killed. The Wabbly clanked and rumbled and roared obliviously past them. Sergeant Walpole saw the flexing springs in the tread-joints, and there were hundreds of them, of a size to support a freight-car. He saw a refuse-tube casually ejecting a gush of malodorous stuff, in which the garbage of a mess-table was plainly identifiable. A drop or two of the stuff splashed on him, and he smelled coffee.

And then the treads lifted, and he saw the monstrous gas-spreading tubes at the stern, and the exhaust-pipes into which he could have ridden, monocycle and all. Then he saw a man in the Wabbly. There were ventilation-ports open at the pointed stern and a man was looking out, some fifteen feet above the ground, smoking placidly and looking out at the terrain the Wabbly left behind it. He was wearing an enemy uniform cap.

The monster went on. The roar of its passing diminished a little. And the 'copter man came suddenly out of the staff-car, struggling with the portable vision set.

"I think we can do it," he said shortly. "It's in constant beam communication with a bomber up aloft, and I think they're worried up there because they can't see a damned thing. But it's a good team. With the Wabbly's beam, which takes so much power no bomber could possibly carry it, the bombers are safe, and the bombers can locate any motor-driven thing that might attack the Wabbly and blow it to hell. But right now they can't see it. So I think we can do it. Coming?"

Sergeant Walpole threw away his cigarette and rose stiffly. Even those few moments of rest had intensified his weariness. He flung a leg over the monocycle's seat and pointed tiredly to the trail of the Wabbly. It nearly paralleled, here, a ribbon of concrete road which once had been a reasonably important feeder-highway.

"Let's go."

They went off through the rain along the road, nearly parallel to the route the Wabbly was taking. Rain beat at them. Off in the woods to their right the Wabbly's noise grew louder as they overtook it. They passed it, and came abruptly out of the wooded area upon cultivated fields, rolling and beautifully cared-for. There had been a farm-headquarters off to one side, a huge central-station for all the agricultural work on what once would have been half a county, but there were jagged walls where buildings had been, and smoke still rose from the place.

Then the Wabbly came out of the woods, a dim gray monstrous shape in the rain.

The helicopter man pulled the ignition-cord and a rocket began to sputter. He made a single wipe with his knife-blade along the twisted insulated wires of the Bissel battery, and a wavering blue spark leaped into being. The rocket shot upward, curved down, and landed with enough force to bury its head in the muddy ploughed earth and conceal the signal-flare that must have ignited.

"That ought to do it," said the 'copter man. "Let's send some more."

Sergeant Walpole got exhaustedly off his monocycle and duplicated the 'copter man's efforts. A second rocket, a third. . . . A dozen or more rockets went off, each one bearing a wavering, uncertain blue spark at its tip. And that spark would continue for half an hour or more. In a loop aerial, eight miles up, it might sound like a spark-plug, or it might sound like something else. But it would not sound like the sort of thing that ought to spring up suddenly in front of the Wabbly, and it would sound like something that had better be bombed, for safety's sake.

The Wabbly was moving across the ploughed fields with a deceptive smoothness. It was drawing nearer and nearer to the spot where the rockets had plunged to earth.

It stopped.

Another rocket left the weary pair of men, its nearly flashless exhaust invisible in the daytime, anyway. The Wabbly backed slowly from the irregular line where the first rockets sparked invisibly. It was no more than a distinct gray shadow in the falling rain, but the queer bulk atop its body moved suddenly. Like a searchlight, the power-beam swept the earth before the Wabbly. But nothing happened.

The 'copter man turned on the vision set he had packed from the staff gyrocar. Voices, crisp and anxious, came out of it. He caressed the set affectionately. "Listen to 'em, Sergeant," he said hungrily. "They're worried!"

The voice changed suddenly. There was a sudden musical buzzing in the set, as of two dozen spitting sparks, in as many tones, all going at once.

"Letting the guys in the Wabbly hear what they hear," said the 'copter man grimly. "If God's good to us, now. . . ."

The voices changed again. They stopped.

The Wabbly itself was still, halted in its passage across a clear and rain-swept field by little sparking sounds which seemed to indicate the presence of something that had better be bombed for safety's sake.

A thin whining noise came down from aloft. It rose to a piercing shriek, and there was a gigantic crater a half mile from the Wabbly, from which smoke rose lazily. The Wabbly remained motionless. Another whining noise which turned to a shriek. . . . The explosion was terrific. It was a bit nearer the Wabbly.

"We'll send 'em some more rockets," said the 'copter man.

They went hissing invisibly through the rain. The Wabbly backed cautiously away from the spot where they landed, because they were wholly invisible and they made a sound which those in the Wabbly could not understand. Always, to a savage, the unexplained is dangerous. Modern warfare has reached the same high peak of wisdom. The Wabbly drew off from the sparks because it could not know what made them, and because it had used its power-beam and the bomber had dropped its bombs without stopping or destroying them. It was not conceivable to anybody on either the Wabbly or the bombers aloft that inexplicable things could be especially contrived to confront the Wabbly, unless they were contrived to destroy it.

"They don't know what in hell they're up against," said the 'copter man joyously. "Now lets give 'em fits!"

Rockets went off in swift succession. To the blinded men in the bomber above the clouds it seemed that unexplained mechanisms were springing into action by dozens, all about the Wabbly. They were mechanisms. They were electric mechanisms. They were obviously designed to have some effect on the Wabbly. And the Wabbly had no defense against the unguessed-at effects of unknown weapons except. . . .

Bombs began to rain from the sky. The Wabbly crawled toward the last gap left in the ring of mysterious mechanisms. That closed. Triumphant, singing sparks sang viciously in the amplifiers. Nothing was visible. Nothing! Perhaps that was what precipitated panic. The bombers rained down their deadly missiles. And somebody forgot the exact length of time it takes a bomb to drop eight miles. . . .

Sergeant Walpole and the 'copter man were flat on the ground with their hands to their ears. The ground bucked and smote them. The unthinkable violence of the hexynitrate explosions tore at their nerves, even at their sanity. And then there was an explosion with a subtle difference in its sound. Sergeant Walpole looked up, his head throbbing, his eyes watering, dizzy and dazed, and bleeding at the nose and ears.

Then he bumped into the 'copter man, shuddering on the ground. He did it deliberately. There was a last crashing sound, and some of the blasted earth spattered on them. But then the 'copter man looked where Sergeant Walpole pointed dizzily.

The Wabbly was careened crazily on one side. One of its treads was uncoiling slowly from its frame. Its stern was blown in. Someone had forgotten how long it takes a bomb to drop eight miles, and the Wabbly had crawled under one. More, from the racked-open stern of the Wabbly there was coming a roaring, spitting cloud of gas. The Wabbly's storage-tanks of gas had been set off. Inside, it would be a shambles. Its crew would be dead, killed by the gas the Wabbly itself had broadcast in its wake. . . .

PART VII

". . . It is a point worth noticing, by any student of strategy, that while the Wabbly in working solely for effectiveness in lowering civilian morale worked upon sound principles, yet the destruction of the Wabbly by Sergeant Walpole and Flight Cadet Ryerson immediately repaired all the damage done. Had it worked toward more direct military aims, its work would have survived it. It remains a pretty question for the student, whether the Enemy Command, with the information it possessed, made the soundest strategic use of its unparalleled weapon. . . . But on the whole, the raid of the Wabbly remains the most startling single strategic operation of the war, if only because of its tremendous effect upon civilian morale. . . ." (*Strategic Lessons of the War of 1941–43.* — U. S. War College. Pp. 94–96.)

A major-general climbed out of a staff gyrocar and waded through mud for half a mile, after which he, in person, waked two sleeping men. They were sprawled out in the puddle of rain which had gathered in a torn-away tread from the Wabbly. They waked with extreme reluctance, and then yawned even in the act of saluting in a military manner.

"Yes, sir," said Sergeant Walpole, yawning again. "Yes, sir; the bombers've gone. We heard 'em tryin' to raise the Wabbly for about half an hour after she'd blown up. Then they cut off. I think they went home, sir. Most likely, sir, they think we used some new dinkus on the Wabbly. It ain't likely they'll realize they blew it up themselves for us."

The major-general gave crisp orders. Men began to explore the Wabbly, cautiously. He turned back to the two sleepy and disreputable men who had caused its destruction. His aspect was one of perplexity and admiration.

"What did you men do?" he demanded warmly. "What in hell did you do?"

Sergeant Walpole grinned tiredly. The 'copter man spoke for him.

"I think, sir," said the helicopter man, "that we affected the morale of the Wabbly's and the bombers' crews."

GROOVES

The sun was pouring down heat, and the whole valley felt like a furnace. Little eddies of hot wind touched us languidly now and then, not refreshing us, not even adding to our discomfort, but merely emphasizing the heat and dryness of our surroundings. We sat on the rough-planked porch of Martin's saloon and looked up the valley, watching the trail quiver and seem to rock in the heat.

"No," said Jimmy Calton, continuing the discussion he had been carrying on entirely by himself. "Th' trouble with people is that they don't see what's just before their noses. They go round lookin' for somethin' excitin' that ain't there."

He lounged carelessly in his chair, expertly flicking the ashes from his cigarette into the floppy wide ear of a huge yellow dog that slept peacefully stretched out on the floor. When the ashes struck the dog's ear, he would lazily flick them out and go back to sleep again.

I mumbled something indistinguishable in answer to Jimmy's pronouncement. Heat always takes all the energy out of me and I revert to my normal state of utter indolence. Jimmy took my mumble as a sign of interest, however, and continued his remarks.

"'Most everybody," he said didactically, "goes around callin' himself *Sherlock Holmes* or *Nick Carter*. Everybody's got a habit o' thinkin' in a groove o' mystery. Everybody thinks the same thing every time. Nobody likes anything he can't make into a mystery."

"Don't like things they can understand?" I queried listlessly. "How's that? I don't agree with you."

"Shuh!" Jimmy flicked a bit of ash accurately into the yellow dog's ear. The dog reproachfully sat up and scratched it out with his hind foot, then lay down again.

"Shuh!" Jimmy repeated. "Why, looka here. S'pose you're ridin' on a trolley-car in Houston an' are hangin' onto a strap. Right in front of you is a pale, puny-lookin' sort of feller, pale-faced, lookin' like a girl. He's got curly hair that needs cuttin' and he don't seem never to have needed a shave. He's got small hands, an' his ears're small an' nice-lookin'. You, danglin' on a strap like they do on the streetcars in Houston, you've got a bundle in your hand. You see this guy lookin' up at you. He's got blue eyes, awful blue eyes, like you always think the girl you're in love with has got."

"I never do," I defended myself. "I always fall in love with brunettes."

"Any way you like," Jimmy conceded. "But you're standin' up there in front of this guy, an' you've got a bundle in your hand. Th' car goes around a corner sudden, an' your bundle drops in this guy's lap. Instead of closin' his knees together to catch it, he throws 'em apart. What would you think?"

"I don't understand," I said.

Jimmy pulled his bag of makings out of his pocket and tossed it into my lap. Instinctively, I closed my knees upon it to keep it from falling to the floor.

"Oh," I said. "Everybody knows a man puts his knees together to make a lap and a woman throws hers apart. That's because she wears a skirt."

"Well, what would you think if this guy on the streetcar threw his apart? Remember, he's pale, an' puny, an' sort o' hunched over."

"I'd say he was a woman masquerading in men's clothes," I said promptly.

Jimmy nodded his head.

"O' course you'd say that," he admitted. "I did hope you might have more sense, but it's all right."

"Well, what should I think?" I demanded. I was a little nettled by Jimmy's manner. He is a decent sort of fellow and has given me a lot of good stories, but there is no use denying that he is irritating sometimes.

"He might be a shoemaker," Jimmy suggested mildly. "They wear leather aprons, an' have to hol' scraps o' leather an' things in 'em, so they spread their knees to make laps to hol' things in. Ain't it true? An' wouldn't that account for his bein' hunched over, an' all that?"

I grunted in ungraceful admission of my defeat and relapsed into silence. We sat without speech for some moments. All the valley was very quiet. The heat made everything seem to dance in jerky, hypnotic motions. Inside the bar we could hear the flies buzzing dully about. Occasionally a half-strangled snore came from within. Joe, the bartender, lay peacefully behind the bar, resting against the night and the need for labor. Our two ponies dozed against the hitching-rail. Now and then one of them lazily whisked at the numberless flies with his tail, but nearly all of the valley seemed as indolent and as inert as the two of us sitting on the perch. Jimmy sprawled in his chair and fanned himself slowly with his sombrero, puffing the while on his cigarette. The big yellow dog lay soundly asleep in the strange languor of hot climates.

"It ain't to be wondered at," Jimmy said presently, referring to his former subject of conversation. "When folks had to think things out f'r themselves they diden' stick to grooves, but now — gosh! Look at Joe inside there. The barkeep that was here before him knowed every man in forty miles real intimate, an' most men in four hundred miles well enough to lend 'em money. He knowed every brand, an' every ranch, an' most Mexes well enough to keep the wrong ones out o' here. An' look at Joe. What d'you s'pose he'd do 'f I asked him where Carey Walters lives? He'd use th' telephone!"

"Not that bad," I said. "Everybody knows where Carey lives."

"Pretty near that bad," Jimmy repeated doggedly. "He'd call up somebody that knowed an' ask how to get there from here. He thinks in a groove, a telephone groove. Everybody thinks in grooves nowadays."

He threw the butt of his cigarette away and sat in disgusted silence. Without energy to stir him up again, I lay lazily back and looked out at a dazzling world through half-closed eyes. The sun-glare was terrific. The whole valley seemed to be simply baking slowly but thoroughly in the hot, pitiless sunshine. Presently, far down the quivering, baking track that through courtesy we called a road, a whirl of dust appeared, and then a darker spot in its center.

"Here comes somebody," I said without movement. "Must be Carey."

Jimmy squinted his eyes and watched the approaching figure.

"Yeah," he said. "He ought to have better sense than to travel in the middle of the day."

"I wonder," I said idly, "if his wife is standing up well in the heat."

"I saw her a couple of weeks ago," Jimmy yawned, "and she looked pretty well. He's a lucky dog. She's *una muy gallina,* believe me!"

That was Jimmy's private Spanish rendition of "Some chicken!" He had a habit of translating American slang into 'dobe Spanish and inflicting it upon his hearers. In this case, he happened to be quite correct. Mary Walters was one of the most charming little women a fool husband ever dragged away from civilization. Her husband was the manager of a tiny mine ten miles from everywhere but the saloon on whose porch we sat. With the sublime folly of an adoring husband, he had brought his wife there, to live in the manager's house, to be the only white woman in thirty miles, and to almost literally fry in the heat of the valley. There were thirty or forty Mex women attached to the village of the mine-workers, and about seventy-five or so men about the mine, but her husband was the only white man she would see for weeks on end. He usually had a white assistant, but for two months past had been without one.

"He shouldn't have taken her up there," I said resentfully. "It's ridiculous to expect a white woman to live like that."

"But he did," Jimmy said lazily. "The point isn't that he shouldn't have taken her there, but just he's got in a groove of thinkin'. He married her. Wives ought to live with their husbands. An' so —"

"He certainly oughtn't leave her there alone," I said virtuously.

"You're right there," Jimmy agreed. "We're no more'n twenty miles from the border."

"I wasn't thinking of raids," I remarked. "The rangers have pretty well taken care of them."

"I was thinkin' of raids," Jimmy was quite serious. "Every spigoty revoltoso in Chihuahua is just lookin' f'r a chanst to make a gran'stan' raid. 'F he c'n make a big splash an' get his name in all the 'dobe newspapers — like the ones that come out once a week an' say Roosevelt is headin' a revolution in the States an' the President's had to move the gov'ment to Canada — a big raid'll mean any number of men f'r him."

"But they wouldn't dare raid this far," I protested. "And no one could get any number of men this far with any hope of getting back."

"Wouldn't need many men," Jimmy persisted. "Half a dozen men 'd be plenty."

"There are seventy-five at the mine," I pointed out.

"And fifty of 'em 'd join the raiders," Jimmy replied casually. "You don't know greasers yet. I ain't sayin' there's any real danger. I'd have licked some sense into Carey 'f I'd thought there was, an' I wouldn't be loafing here, either. I just said it was possible. Those spigoties think in grooves, too. But you know the Mariposita is a dam' rich mine if it is small. It'd be worth takin' a chance on. I'd raid it myself f'r much."

Carey waved his hat to us and drew up before the door.

"Hello, people," he said cheerfully, and mounted the steps. "Come in and have a drink."

We followed him. Joe, inside, woke reluctantly and served us, then lay down again to sleep.

"I'm going to use the telephone, Joe," Carey said matter-offactly, and went to the instrument. We heard him call his wife and give her a message to be delivered to the Mex foreman.

"Carey," said Jimmy deliberately when he turned away, "what's eatin' you, goin' aroun' in this hot weather?"

"I got a phone call that the owners are down in Dos Pasos and want to see me. They don't want to come out to the mine. I don't blame them," he added with a laugh. "It's some ride even this far, and it's going to be worse the rest of the way."

"You got a telephone out there at the mine now?" Jimmy asked curiously. "You musta had money to burn to run a wire all that ways."

Carey laughed again.

"The owners put it in, and I wanted it for Mary, anyway. She was getting a little bit lonesome, and having a phone in is almost like being in town."

"Of course," Jimmy said with a trace of sarcasm. Carey did not notice.

"You ought to see the way the mine is turning out," he said in a burst of enthusiasm. "You know what placer stuff is like, but this is a wonder! I'm carrying down some stuff that will open the owners' eyes."

"You carryin' around a lot of stuff casual like?" Jimmy asked. "An' all by yourself?"

"I've got more than I like to think about," Carey admitted. "It's all right, though. Nobody'll bother me. The men expect me to carry down the month's output next week and get the money for their pay. They'll never suspect I'm going to trot down with it today. I'll get back by tomorrow night with their pay and then I don't mind their finding out. This is the best plan, after all."

Jimmy looked a trifle queer, but said nothing. In a moment or two more Carey mounted again and rode away.

"Grooves," said Jimmy meditatively as he disappeared down the valley. "Grooves. There was a guy once wrote a thing — a story or somethin' — sayin' that the best way to hide a thing was to not hide it at all."

"'The Purloined Letter'," I suggested.

"I don't know." Jimmy's brow was wrinkled. "I ain't much on readin'. But that story thing makes more trouble than most any one other thing I know. It started a new kind o' groove. Look at Carey there. Everybody that bothers to think about it at all will know he's carryin' somethin' to show the owners. See? It's near th' time to carry the stuff, he's got a lot of it, an' he's got to go to town. He wouldn't want to leave all that unguarded at the mine anyway."

"You just said that thinking in grooves — and having a guard with him would be thinking in grooves — was the worst thing a man could do. You're contradicting yourself."

"That shows I'm tellin' the truth," Jimmy said cryptically. "When a man is lyin' he's pretty sure to be plausible. When he contradicts himself he knows what he's talking about."

He rolled another cigarette and lighted it, throwing the extinguished match at the head of the sleepy yellow dog on the porch. I lay back in my chair again, and half-closed my eyes. The valley danced and quivered in the heat. The two ponies still dozed at the hitching-rail. I was taking a vacation and had ridden over early in the morning from the ranch at which I was stopping. I had been told I would probably find Jimmy turning up some time during the day, but so far he had merely bored me with didactic reflections on life in general.

Jimmy, as a storyteller, was amusing, but as a philosopher he was dull. I found myself growing more and more drowsy from the heat. A small lizard poked his head from beneath a stumpy bit of yellow brush, heard nothing, and ventured out into the sunlight. He lay still, torpid, basking, baking in the sun. The big yellow dog gave a sigh and flopped his uppermost ear, in which Jimmy had just flicked a bit of cigarette-ash. Jimmy began to speak again, but I paid no attention. A muffled, strangled snore came from inside the house. The sun poured down. A little whirl of hot, dry air touched my face. My soft collar was damp with perspiration.

I lay back, comfortable, my arm lazily hanging down. My cigarette slipped from the relaxed fingers and rolled on the rough plank flooring of the porch. The valley danced dizzily in the heat. I slipped off into that delightful state of half-waking, half-sleeping semi-consciousness that is the true siesta.

I roused with a start. The telephone-bell inside was ringing. I had not dozed long, no more than a normal midday siesta. I heard Joe, inside, shuffle protestingly across the floor to the phone. He took down the receiver and answered it sleepily.

"Naw, he ain't here. He lef' a couple o' hours ago. Jimmy Calton's here. Wan' ter talk to him?"

Jimmy rose, stretched, and went indoors.

"Hello," he said casually into the transmitter. The next second I had a sense of an electric tension. Jimmy's voice had changed entirely.

"You're Mendez? At the Mariposita? What's up?"

I went inside. Jimmy was pale as death. Joe, the bartender, stared at him, puzzled.

"What's the matter, Jimmy?" I asked curiously.

He paid no attention for a moment, listening on the receiver.

"Wait a minute, Mendez," he said quietly, and turned to face us.

"Felipe Mendez is at the Mariposita. He crossed th' border las' night an' made f'r the mine. His gang's in charge now, only they dynamited the safe an' foun' Carey took all the stuff with 'im. Now Mendez says if he don't come back with it, it's good-by for Carey's wife."

He stood still a moment, his fingers working nervously.

"You know what that means," he said sharply. "It'd take hours to catch Carey, an' if he came back, it'd be good-by anyway. There ain't any rangers we can get together in time. Dammit, what're we goin' to do?"

I went to the phone. Some two or three months before I had met Mendez. He was then a strong partisan of the central government, and I had interviewed him. He would remember me, I felt sure, because from motives of policy I had praised him in moderation. I told him who I was and he did remember me.

"What's this Jimmy Calton tells me?" I asked.

"I am sorree," Mendez's oily voice came over the phone. "But to conduct the *revolucion* funds are necessaree. So. But reparation may be had from *el Gobernador*."

"But what's this question of Mrs. Walters?"

"My men, they are much disappointed. I cannot blame them. To hold the *señora* as a hostage is the onlee possible way to secure the funds we must have."

Jimmy suddenly came up behind me and took the receiver from my hand.

"Go get the ponies in shape," he said quietly. "You're game for a scrap? Joe, you're comin', too."

We went out and I, for one, paced nervously up and down. Joe went to the rear of the saloon and reappeared leading a pony. I heard Jimmy still talking inside, but could not distinguish his words. He joined us in a moment and jumped on his horse. We thumped away up the valley in the blistering heat, the hot wind burning our faces. I could not understand what was wanted of me, because I am without exception the worst shot in America. Joe rode sullenly beside me.

"I don't know what we c'n do," Jimmy said wretchedly. "I said we had enough to pay him in the bar safe, an' I'd bring it if Mary Walters wasn't harmed. I talked to her, an' so far she's jus' scared. We gotta trus' t' luck."

"You mean we're goin' t' fight?" asked Joe with a groan. "Hell, I ain't no fighter."

It was very hot in the valley, but I began to feel a little chilly. Riding cold-bloodedly into a fight is not as pleasant a sensation as one would suppose. I began to think of many solemn things. The worst of them was that I would be quite useless.

"We're to ride up to a mile o' Carey's cabin, an' then a couple o' spigoties'll come an' meet me. I'm t' go on alone an' see Mary, an' bring 'er back — presumably," he added grimly. "Looka here, fellers, I got somethin' up m' sleeve, but if I don't get out with her all right —"

Joe grunted. I felt very queer.

"I think I'm goin' to be all right," Jimmy said carefully. "I'm countin' on th' Mexes thinkin' in grooves, too."

We pounded on up the trail, with the blinding dust rising all around us, soaked in sweat and with the dust turning to mud as it settled upon us. Joe rode uncomfortably and ungracefully, but he seemed vastly more comfortable mentally than I was. We were going into a tight place. Mendez was not a pleasant person to deal with. He would probably, as Jimmy had foretold only a few hours before, have only half a dozen or a dozen men with him, but to me that was far too many. It is all very well to talk about one white man being a match for several Mexicans, but — well, I was uncomfortable. In spite of the heat and the sweat that poured from every pore, I felt cold all over. I do not think I was intended to be a hero.

Jimmy seemed to be going over his plan again and again. Neither Joe nor myself knew what it was. We knew Jimmy had promised to bring a ransom for Mary Walters, and we knew he had not brought it — that, in fact, there was no sum of money to bring. Carey had the only really big sum in the locality, and he was miles away and going blissfully along, quite unconscious of his wife's danger. It was quite hopeless, altogether. I had heard some few tales of Mendez, and knew that even if Jimmy did turn over all the money Mendez demanded, Mendez was just as likely as not to shoot him casually and keep Mary Walters as his captive anyway. And the thought of a white woman in the hands of one of Mexico's *revoltoso* chieftains —

Jimmy reined up.

"I'm goin' t' try to hang on to my gun," he said to us, "but 'f I can't, after I've gone up to Carey's house you two edge up as close as you can. An' if there's shootin' — as I expec' — you two come a runnin'."

"Hell!" Joe said mournfully. "I ain't no fighter."

I confess I swallowed hard. My hands were shaking, at any rate, when I reached for the pistol in my hip-pocket. I slipped it into the side-pocket of my coat. Joe did the same. Jimmy was not wearing chaps, merely corduroy trousers above his boots, and he had a big bulge in his hip pocket. He left it there.

We came in sight of Carey's house. It stood by itself on top of a rise in the ground. The mine itself lay over the ridge. We could see one or two of the houses of the mine-workers, but most of them were hidden with the mine. Two men, apparently of Mendez's gang, loafed before the door of Carey's house.

When we appeared there was a stir. The two men before Carey's cottage called inside and the door opened. I recognized Mendez. He grinned at us and gave some orders to the pair. They started down toward us. Two or three men from the village ran up to the house, and received further instructions from Mendez. By this time the two he had first spoken to were quite near.

Jimmy rode forward to meet them. There was an angry argument. The two men were evidently insisting that he surrender his weapons before he came up to the house. At last, with a very ill grace, Jimmy gave in. He handed over his pistol. Even then, however, they were not satisfied. One of them patted his pockets to make sure he had no other weapons. Then they went on up to the house. Mendez greeted Jimmy with a flashing smile, showing his white teeth. Jimmy evidently snapped at him. The pair disappeared indoors.

Joe looked at me uncomfortably. I gripped my pistol nervously and we edged forward. Carey's house seemed to quiver a little in the heat. Our hearts in our throats, we edged our horses toward it. One of the men before the door entered, apparently in response to an order.

There was a sudden yell from the house, and an explosion. We dashed forward recklessly, scared stiff but desperate, going for the house. The men outside ran for the door. One of them stopped and fired at us, but the bullet went wild. They disappeared inside and two more shots sounded. We pounded up to the door, and Jimmy appeared, holding Mary by the arm, a little trickle of blood coming from his ear. He was facing inside with his arm leveled, and he was swearing atrociously in Spanish.

Our arrival seemed to help matters. He unceremoniously handed Mary over to me and, with Joe, went back inside. There was a slight scuffle, but then he came out again and began to wipe the blood off his neck.

"Got 'em," he said in a satisfied tone.

"But, Jimmy," I protested, "how did you do it?"

"Why, I stuck up Mendez as soon's I got inside," he said deliberately, "an' made 'im call one of his gang to come in. I'd tied Mendez up, but when this guy come in he yelled. I had to shoot 'im. Then the others come runnin', an' one of 'em nicked my ear. Th' others played my game's soon's they saw I had 'em covered."

"But they disarmed you," I protested again. "I saw them search you for a pistol."

Jimmy grinned.

"Grooves," he said sententiously. "Grooves. Mexes think in grooves jus' like other folks. You saw that feller feel my pockets?"

"I did," I said.

Jimmy stood up.

"See 'f I've got a gun now," he ordered.

I felt his pockets and shook my head.

"Grooves," said Jimmy pityingly. "You think in grooves, too. I got a gun, the same one I used on th' Mexes. You felt my right pants-pocket, an' my left pants-pocket, an' my hip-pocket, an' my coat-pockets, but you didn't never think that I might be left-handed."

"What's that got to do with it?"

"I got a left hip-pocket," said Jimmy mildly. "Nobody ever puts anything in 'em, but everybody wears 'em. Nobody uses 'em but left-handed people — an' me."

FOOTPRINTS IN THE SNOW

The snow was deep, but not soft. There was enough of cold to keep the snow-crystals brittle and hard. They glistened until they hurt the eyes, and as I trudged along behind my sledge they crackled with a faintly musical tinkle beneath my snow-shoes.

It was not really cold, though. I was almost hot in the heavy clothing I wore, and the dogs loafed on their job. The sled was light enough, in all conscience, but they pulled with hardly half their strength. I did not press them. There was no hurry. I was to meet Pierre Chambour at Three Mile Run that afternoon and it was still early in the morning with our rendezvous a bare dozen miles away.

I had passed the mail-sled the afternoon before and been told of a shorter trail than the one I had intended, so I had time to spare. That must explain my stop at the cabin I saw from the trail. I invented some pretext — I pretended to inquire if this was indeed the proper and shorter trail to Three Mile Run — but I felt queerly ashamed when I entered the place. I mention the cabin because what Pierre told me later made it interesting.

It was tenanted by an old man, obviously an invalid, who lay back in an improvised easy chair, and an animal that moved about laboriously on twisted and crippled limbs. The face of the old man was a proud one, with strangely scornful eyes, and I instinctively began to stammer out an apology for intruding, in spite of my knowledge that visitors are welcome in any of the French-Canadian cabins of the backwoods.

The old man looked at me scornfully, and the animal began to hobble toward me with a snarl. It was a wolf, whose body was whole and sound, and whose head and jaws were ferocious and well-muscled, but whose limbs had at some time been cruelly broken and unskillfully healed. It was barely able to progress across the floor by means of effortful contortions, and surely would not have been formidable, but I was spared the need of defending myself against its intended attack by the entrance of a girl from another room.

With a gesture she halted the wolf and bade me welcome. I completed my apology for intruding and asked if I were on the right trail.

"Yes, *m'sieu'*," she said gravely. "There is but the one trail, once you have branched from the main way."

"Thank you," I said, and hesitated. "Er — you have a queer pet," I added helplessly.

It is not customary to ask a question and depart without further words in the Canadian backwoods. One is usually expected to stay and gossip. These people, however, evidently had no such expectation. The girl bent down and picked up the cruelly misshapen creature from the floor and carried it over to a cushion by the fireplace, where it lay and looked at me steadily.

"Yes, *m'sieu'*," she said quietly. She glanced up. "I am sure," she added with perfect courtesy, "that *m'sieu'* will have no further trouble with the trail."

I found myself outside the cabin, flushing slightly. Her intimation that I was not expected to stay was unmistakable, but there had been no discourtesy in her tone. It had been rather the symbol of an invincible reserve.

When I realized that fact I remarked to myself that I had no faintest desire to pry into her affairs and mushed on along behind my dog-team. All the same, the whole thing puzzled me. That animal, crippled in that way, that proud-faced old man, and the girl who so politely showed me the door.

Thinking it over, I was struck by an expression I had noticed on her face. Once in a great while you see a face which is at once unutterably sad and quite tranquil. Most often you see that expression on the faces of women who have retired from the world for reasons which are between themselves and their Maker, and devoted themselves to prayer.

That was the expression I had seen on her face. Past agony which could never be forgotten, but palliated by later and continued peace. I made a mental note to ask Pierre about her, and continued on my way.

Pierre was waiting for me. I saw the smoke of his fire some distance away, and his dogs and mine were greeting each other with loud defiances long before I saw Pierre himself. He is a friend I value highly, in spite of the efforts of worthy people to set me against him.

His silvery hair has not been lightened in vain. He is wise in the things not taught in books, and he has taught me some of his lore. At the same time, he is a rich mine of queer fancies and occasionally grotesque superstitions. Almost the first thing he did was to show me a fresh wolfskin, which he told me he had shot.

"And it is very hard to shoot a wolf, *m'sieu*," he explained, "especially when food is as plentiful as now. They know rifles when they see them and will not show themselves."

His statement did not surprise me. I had heard many tales of wolves and their knowledge and cunning. In fact, one of the reasons I wanted to see Pierre was to get his opinion of a theory I had formed that the legends of werewolves that are found wherever wolves have been, are due to the almost or quite human intelligence of the brutes. I asked Pierre how he had shot the animal whose skin he was displaying.

He told me with great detail precisely how he came to be certain that a wolf was hiding from his rifle behind a certain copse, of how he had made it impossible for the wolf to slink away unseen, and how a supremely lucky shot had brought down the animal as it made a dash for the brushwood that would hide it.

"The merit of the shot," said Pierre humbly, "is undoubtedly due to the aid of the Virgin of Etretat, whose relic I wear. She was ever the benefactor of all travelers."

By that time I was busily arranging my camp beside his own, so he did not see me smile at the idea of heavenly intervention in favor of such a hardened old reprobate as himself. Instead, he went on to tell me wonderful anecdotes in which his reliquary figured; notably, instances in which it had aided people in danger from wolves and other wild animals, but mostly wolves.

It was a curious relic in itself, undoubtedly antique, and I knew that either from the sense of security it gave him or from some other cause he was utterly fearless where wolves were concerned. More than once he had appeared with litters of furry, snarling wolf cubs to sell to wild-animal dealers, and the securing of wolf cubs is not an enterprise to be undertaken by the nervous.

When I had fed my dogs and settled down to the preparation of supper, it had grown quite dark. I anticipated some trouble in getting my share of firewood, but Pierre had enough for both and we were soon swallowing mugs of steaming tea to top off our meal. We filled our pipes, and when Pierre had settled comfortably back and his pipe was drawing well, I started to explain my theory of the origin of werewolf tales.

Taken in itself, it sounded plausible enough. Consider an animal clever enough to attack an unarmed man and hide itself at sight of a man with a rifle. Or an animal capable of a degree of comradeship which would lead it, itself secure, to leap out of hiding and risk its life to rescue a comrade in difficulties.

Multiply those two instances by a thousand others, each evidencing an intelligence almost incredible. Think of the fact that in three years they learned what poison meant, so that it is practically impossible to poison a wolf nowadays. That they learned what rifles meant and what they did not mean.

Is it surprising that an animal displaying such cunning should in times past have been credited with possessing a human brain — of being, in fact, a human being metamorphosed? It would be astonishing if they had not.

I put forward my theory with a great deal of enthusiasm. Pierre listened with flattering attention, but when I finished he shook his head. I noticed that he reached his hand inside his shirt, and I think it was to take a comforting grasp of the reliquary suspended about his neck by a cord.

"No, *m'sieu'*," he said firmly. "I do not think your idea is right."

It nettled me a little.

"Have you a better explanation, then?" I asked, somewhat unamiably.

His face was very grave.

"I have, *m'sieu*. My explanation is that the legends are true."

My face must have expressed my amazement and amusement. At any rate, Pierre cast a glance behind him and took a fresh grasp of his reliquary.

"M'sieu'," he said earnestly, "let me beg of you that you will not laugh at such dangerous subjects. It is not wise. I — I assure you it is not wise. If I were not secure in the protection of the Virgin of Etretat, I would not dare even discuss it like this."

I stared at him in some astonishment.

"But, Pierre," I protested. "You don't believe that foolishness! You don't believe that there are people who turn into wolves, or wolves that turn into people!"

Pierre puffed silently on his pipe for a moment or so. He seemed to be debating something within himself, and the debate caused him a little nervousness. Suddenly, however, he rapped the ashes out of his pipe and said decisively:

"M'sieu', I shall tell you how Jean Lenoir came to his death, and you may decide for yourself what I believe. I knew Jean Lenoir, in fact, I — we — that is — there was some difficulty with the government in which we were both involved at the same time."

Knowing Pierre, I made a shrewd guess that they had both been suspected of selling whisky to the Indians, which suspicion was quite likely to be well founded. I waited for the story.

"It does not seem well, *m'sieu'*," said Pierre after a pause, "it does not seem well at all, since he is dead, to say that Jean Lenoir was an evil man, but his name was a fit description, though an accident. *Lenoir*, you understand, in our language means 'the black.'

"I do not think I should speak ill of the dead, but Jean was truly evil as no other man I have known was evil — and I have known many evil men. A huge, black-bearded man, *m'sieu'*, with arms like one of the great monkeys of which Du Challu writes. A monstrous man, with a huge chest and the neck of a bull. And most of all, the rage of a lion. Men trembled at the roar of his voice when they knew nothing of him, but they fled when they knew of his repute.

"Imagine a man always a brute, and ten thousand devils when drunk. Imagine a man whose strength was such that no man dared oppose him, and whose skill with his weapons was such that though six men had fallen at his hands there was no one brave enough to attempt to bring him to justice. Think of a man who knew no law save his own passions, and whose terrible strength enabled him to enforce that law without mercy and without respite. Sometimes, *m'sieu'*, I wonder that I risked my life to associate with him in any enterprise."

Pierre half sighed. Looking at the white-haired old sinner, with his gentle voice, one was tempted to wonder at his reputation for daring. It took closer acquaintance to reveal the cause.

"He is dead," said Pierre thoughtfully, "and the manner of his death leaves but little doubt as to the fate he met in the afterworld, but somehow I am not filled with sorrow. The good curé tells me I should pray for the souls of all that are dead, and so I do. *Le bon Dieu* knows Jean Lenoir needs prayers.

"Somehow I think of a little wolf-cub I gave him once. He admired its spirit, *m'sieu'*, among a litter I had caught to sell to the dealers, as I do sometimes. This one had pushed aside all its brothers and sisters to secure the warmest place by the fire for itself. It snarled at me when I would have moved it. And Jean Lenoir laughed hugely at it, *m'sieu'*, and asked me to give it to him.

"I gave it. One does not refuse gifts to such as Jean. He petted it for perhaps two weeks, and then he cursed it while in drink, and it sank its teeth in his hand."

Pierre's lips tightened.

"What did he do?" I asked.

"He broke it, *m'sieu'*," said Pierre simply. "He cracked the tiny bones of its limbs in his hands until the little thing could not walk or stand, and then he cast it out in the snow. I would have shot it, but Estelle Duval found it by the side of the trail and took it to her home. It would have been kinder to have killed it, but she strove to cure it."

"Was that the crippled thing that crawled about the floor of the cabin back on the trail?"

"You stopped in there?" asked Pierre. "Yes, that is the cub, now grown. A fit companion for Marcel Duval. There is more of Jean's devilment. Not Marcel himself. A tree fell upon him and crushed him, so that he sits always in a chair and suffers. He needs drugs to make him sleep. I spoke of Estelle."

"How?" I asked. "She had a strange expression —"

"The devilment of Jean. He should have suffered a thousand deaths for that, though the death he died was horrible." Pierre shivered a little. He had seemed lost in his story, but his faint uneasiness reappeared for a moment, only to vanish again as he went on.

"I said that Jean was a brute at all times, and ten thousand devils when drunk. Only a devil would have done what he did. *M'sieu'*, you saw that household. The father an invalid, the watch-dog a pitifully maimed, tame wolf, and the girl Estelle. You saw how slim, how frail, how tiny she is to bear the burden of maintaining that *ménage?*"

I nodded.

"Jean Lenoir was drunk," said Pierre, with the hurried speech of one who hastens to be rid of a distasteful incident. "He came down that trail, ten thousand devils alive in him. He saw the light in the window of the cabin.

"He entered. The father helpless, the wolf helpless, and Estelle — you saw Estelle."

"I did," I said angrily.

"That was Jean Lenoir's work." Pierre waved his hand. "When he left — he was not merciful. He did not kill her."

"And you let the man live?" I demanded furiously. "You did not kill him? And you called yourselves men?"

Pierre smiled apologetically. He is an amiable person, and as a friend I value him highly, but I would not like to have him for an enemy. There is a streak of pure, unadulterated villainy in him.

"You forget that Jean was the equal of ten men in combat, and a deadly shot with his rifle. No one dared seize him. If Estelle had had a lover, or a brother — But her father was an invalid."

I eyed Pierre with something less than my former liking. He went on imperturbably.

"I see you are not pleased with me, *m'sieu'*, but you must remember that at that time I was not in favor with the government. I was one of the few men who dared visit Jean's cabin. If I slew him, I would have been accused of murder, and to think of delivering him alive was madness.

"My sympathy was all with Estelle, as it is now —" and the

old reprobate paused a moment while endeavoring to squeeze out a crocodile-tear — "but my hands were tied. I thank *le bon Dieu* that I did not stay with Jean in his cabin, but then, as now, I wore the reliquary of the Virgin of Etretat, and it is due to her that I am alive today."

"You spoke of a werewolf," I said somewhat coldly.

"But yes, *m'sieu*. A werewolf in very truth. You know the form the — the — they take?" Pierre was defiantly going on with his story, despite his knowledge of my disappointment in him, and his nervous dread of speaking of werewolves.

"They appear to a man sometimes as a beautiful woman, who smiles upon him, rousing all his passions. And when the man would seize the figure before him, it yields to his embrace until his throat is exposed. And then the man is found the next day with his throat torn out, and men say a wolf crept upon him while he slept. You have heard of such things?"

"The tale is familiar," I said grudgingly.

"Upon all nights but one they may not deceive any man who recites the charm against werewolves — which I do, *m'sieu'*, at the proper times. But there is one night which is their night, and on that night, wherever they make their appearance, there is great danger.

"On that night I do not open the door of my cabin, *m'sieu'*, no, not though the voice of my best friend called to me from without, for werewolves often take upon themselves the likeness of those we love and trust. On every night but one I fear nothing, but that night I tremble.

"It was on that night, three years ago, that Jean Lenoir heard a soft laugh outside his door and opened it. And there entered his cabin a woman of beauty we may only guess at."

Pierre grasped his reliquary firmly, and for once lost his assurance.

"*M'sieu'*," he said desperately, "you may not believe me, but I tell you of things I saw with these two eyes. I came by the cabin of Jean Lenoir the morning after the Night of the Werewolves.

"His door was open. Leading into that door, and again leading out of it, I saw on the snow the prints of a woman's feet. A woman's feet, *m'sieu'*; not wolf-tracks, but the prints of a *woman's* feet!"

"Well, what of it?" I asked.

Pierre half glanced behind him.

"Jean Lenoir lay on the floor of his cabin," he said nervously. "And his throat had been torn out by the fierce teeth of a wolf. He lay there on the floor of his cabin, and he had not struggled, for nothing was disarranged.

"There were even two glasses still on the table where Jean had sat and drunk with the thing that came to him in the guise of a woman. And in one of the glasses was the dried, caked, whitish slobber of the thing that had drunk with Jean."

"You are sure it was a wolf that had killed him?" I asked.

"I am sure that no jaws but those of a wolf could have torn out his throat like that," said Pierre. The old sinner was surely in earnest. "*M'sieu'*, I swear to you that no wolf-tracks led into that cabin, only the prints of a woman's feet. I swear it, *m'sieu'*. I — I swear it by the Virgin of Etretat.

"And Jean Lenoir lay on the floor of his cabin with his throat torn out by a wolf. That is how he died, *m'sieu'*, and I — I believe in werewolves."

I puffed at my pipe a while in silence. Suddenly an idea came to me.

"Er, Pierre," I said irreverently. "Did you say that Marcel Duval — the invalid, you know — did you say he had to take drugs to make him sleep?"

"Why — yes, *m'sieu'*. What has that to do with my story?"

"Nothing." I continued to smoke in silence. But there came before my eyes as in a vision, the picture of Estelle Duval making her way to Jean Lenoir's cabin on the Night of the Werewolves, carrying a heavy, breathing bundle in her arms.

I seemed to see her enter the cabin. I seemed to see her making merry with Jean Lenoir, drinking with him. And I seemed to see her drop a whitish powder in his drink, such as would later seem to Pierre the dried, caked slobber of the werewolf.

Then Jean Lenoir — or the picture of him I had formed in my mind — seemed to grow sleepy and tumble to the floor. And then the bundle that Estelle Duval had brought crept forward. It was a wolf, whose body was whole and sound, and whose head and jaws were ferocious and well-muscled, but whose limbs had at one time been cruelly broken and unskillfully healed.

It hobbled toward the stupefied Jean Lenoir, while Estelle Duval looked on with a fierce joy in her eyes. The vision faded, but suddenly I realized the reason of the tranquility and the peace that overlay the tragedy in Estelle Duval's eyes.

"*M'sieu'*," said Pierre with uneasy insistence. "Does your theory explain the death of Jean Lenoir, or am I right? Could it have been anything but a werewolf?"

I rapped the ashes out of my pipe.

"No-o, Pierre," I said slowly. "I don't see how it could."

www.ingramcontent.com/pod-product-compliance
Lightning Source LLC
Chambersburg PA
CBHW050801250626
47155CB00005B/2162